neil grant was born in Glasgow, Scotland in the Year of the Fire Horse. He is a kneeboarder who needs to surf more often than he does. His long involvement with the ocean and the difficult business of struggling from boyhood to manhood (almost there) led him to write about these things.

His first novel, *Rhino Chasers*, was published in 2002. He is currently working as a writer/joiner.

NEIL GRANT

INDO DREAMING

ALLEN&UNWIN

First published in 2005

Allen & Unwin
83 Alexander Street
Crows Nest NSW 2065
Australia
Phone: (61 2) 8425 0100
Fax: (61 2) 9906 2218
Email: info@allenandunwin.com
Web: www.allenandunwin.com

National Library of Australia
Cataloguing-in-Publication entry:
Grant, Neil, 1966– .
Indo dreaming.

ISBN 1 74114 179 6.

1. Young men – Fiction. 2. Surfers – Fiction. 3. Male
friendship – Fiction. 4. Indonesia – Fiction. I. Title.

A823.4

Design by Ellie Exarchos
Map of Indonesia by Verity Prideaux
Set in 10/16 Electra by Midland Typesetters
Printed by McPherson's Printing Group

For Ingrid, Emma & Matisse
and our dreams.

Indonesia

INDONESIA

SULAWESI

KALIMANTAN

JAVA

SUMATRA

INDIAN OCEAN

TIMOR
ADONARA
LEMBATA
PANTAR
ALOR
ROTI
SOLOR
Lamalera
Larantuka
Maumere
Labuhanbajo
FLORES
KOMODO
RINCA
Bajawa
SUMBA
Dompu
Sape
Huu
Lakey Beach
SUMBAWA
Sembalun Lawang
Gunung Rinjani
Senaru
LOMBOK
BALI
Denpasar
Kuta
Uluwatu
Bukit Peninsula
Yogyakarta
Parangtritis
Jakarta

MENTAWAIS
NIAS
BANYAK ARCHIPELAGO
Singkil

north

Sharks are designed to kill. When they attack, they flip covers over their eyes, their teeth flex outwards, they can swallow anything. The one that got Castro shredded his board, tore up the water and then dropped back into the shadows of the Southern Ocean.

I saw Castro die.

A week later the postcards started. One a month – pictures of Indonesian breaks, steep peaks over sharp coral. All signed: Castro.

My dead friend is sending me postcards. It's like a voice from hell.

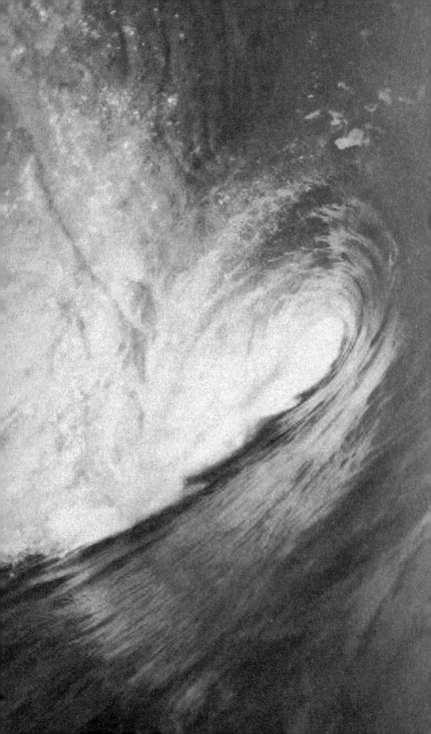

AUSTRALIA

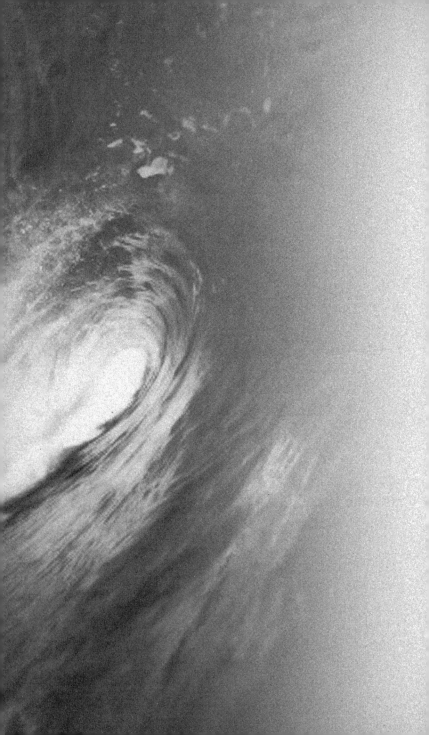

1 Cold water curse

Margaret River, Western Australia

Dreaming of warm water isn't enough; you have to live it. Tucked in the nose of my boardbag is my ticket to paradise. But there is time for one last cold water surf before I fly out tonight.

I have been here just long enough to know this secret spot. The left-hander that burls over sand-covered reef. Winter-stripped grapevines crossing the hills like corduroy. Seals that twist under my board and surface, soft-eyed, to check me out.

The currents around here swirl down from below Indonesia, but there is a touch of Antarctic ice in them, too. A splash of Southern Ocean that makes a steamer a good idea at this time of year. I am out the back with one other guy, watching the grey seam where the ocean meets the sky. Waiting.

This swell was born in a deep ocean storm; its lines pushing out in rings, seeking shallow water to explode into. The northern edge of the rings would have hit Indo – Bali, Java, Lombok, maybe even as far west as Sumatra or as far east as Sumba. The southern swell motored through the ocean until it fell on us; ripping along the broad, sandy beaches, tearing kelp from the sea floor and stranding it in long, leathery strips on the high tide mark.

The guy next to me rolls his board over and picks at a ding near the fin. He slaps the water. 'Come on, Huey!' he shouts at the surf god.

The swell is dying but we are trying to hold onto the last of it. Desperate to suck the last bit of marrow from the bone. It was epic this morning – six foot and glassy as. There were twenty guys out. Now there are only two of us, squabbling over the occasional three-footers that dribble in.

'Man, if I had the dosh I'd be outta here.' The guy planes his hand over the water. 'First flight to Denpasar.'

I nod. It feels wrong to tell him about my trip, like I am pissing on his parade.

'Nearly got there last winter. Had the bucks and everything. Then my mate gets himself busted and can't get a visa. Loser.' He wipes his nose on his wettie sleeve. 'Whaddabout you? Ever been to Indo?'

Shaking my head, I say, 'Nuh.'

'Why not, mate? It's there. Close as close can be. It's your bloody duty to go. It's every Aussie surfer's patriotic bloody duty.' He shifts gear. 'You're not from around here, are ya?'

'Torquay.'

'East-coaster, eh. What you doin over this side then?'

I smile at the sky and wonder where to start. With Castro and his big plans back at Torquay, or in the Bight where I saw him dissolve into the shark-filled water? It just isn't that simple a story. What about Aldo? The Neo-Nazi, the dickhead, the tough man who turned into a boy when it all flew apart. Who we only needed for his car but who I ended up mothering halfway to Margaret River. And Jasper – the hitchhiker who slipped like a shadow into our lives. Where does he fit in? It's like a jigsaw with no picture, no box.

'Just came to surf,' I say to the guy. It is a surfer's answer, waves being more important than the rest of life put together.

He shrugs. 'Long way to come for a wave, but.'

'So's Indo,' I point out.

'Yeah, but *what* waves, buddy. The way they peel off them reefs. Warm spray fanning off the tops.'

This was how Castro had tricked me. This half-dreamy talk, like a hypnotist. And tonight I will be on a plane to try to reach his ghost. A ghost that snuck by us in the Bight and drifted north. A ghost that surfs and writes postcards and hovers above my cold pillow at night so I wake with a dry throat and search the dark room for traces of him.

He is still tricking me.

The guy nods at a wave. 'Yours, mate.'

I stroke deep, two hard pulls, and as soon as I feel the shunt, I jump to my feet. It's nudging four foot, trying hard to barrel, the final fling of the storm. I drag my hand across the face, watching a shoal of whitebait needle through it. As we hit the shallow spot in the reef, the wave feathers and spits and the light fringe of foam at its crest thickens and rolls up and over me. I reach down and grab the nose of my board, holding it tight to the steep wall, foam shooting lightly over my head. The gunmetal sky appears briefly through the roof of water.

Then everything stops. Like the pause button has been pressed. Then rewind, and it's over a year ago at *Thirteenth* – me, Castro and Aldo having an arvo session. That was where it all began – when that cold water cursed us. Castro had dreamed of Indo forever but it was cold water that sealed the deal and forced us from home.

And like that day at *Thirteenth*, the tube shuts down. And I hit the sand and swallow mouthfuls of water and long strands of my own hair. And I think as I spin and scrape along the sea floor about how easy it would be if it all ended here. But then I am up and into the air and grabbing big breaths of the stuff. And I look towards the beach, to where my ticket and my boardbag and my too-new backpack wait. And I paddle in.

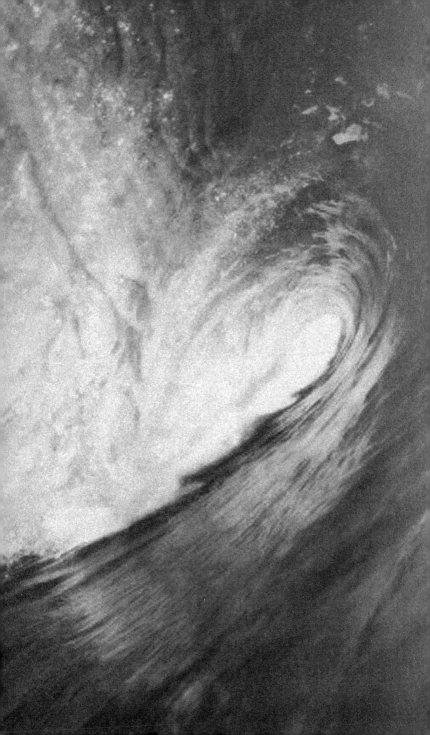

EASTERN ISLANDS

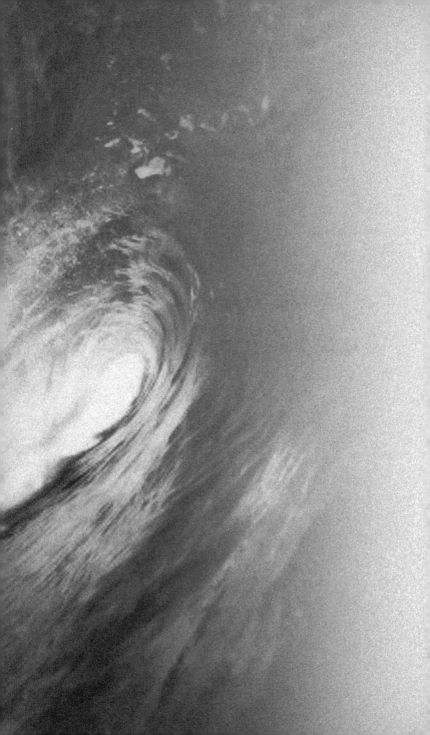

2 Niagara Falls

Kupang, West Timor

Indonesia is wrong. I am wrong. The maimed dogs and beggars and open drains and smoke from burning plastic are all wrong. This dried-up-chicken-wing-and-fly restaurant is way too wrong.

I am watching flies root on my chicken and rice. There is a plastic jug of water and a chipped plastic tumbler in front of me and I am gagging for a drink. There are a billion and one bacteria hanging in the line-up, waiting for me to sip. I will die of thirst before I lift that jug.

Everything in this country scares me and I am shitting bricks about this restaurant. Instead of asking for a cold Coke, I sit like a stunned mullet while the waiter off-loads a plate of chicken on my table. I stare at his singlet – a map of yellow stain-islands – to search for a way out, but he just smiles his buck-toothed smile and leaves me alone with this cold gristle and bullet-hard rice.

My traveller's cheques weigh a thousand kilos. A year of hard labour at Custard Sam's Backpackers paid for them – scrubbing showers, washing crusty sheets; me statue-still as a thousand people came and went, their languages echoing off me. I sold my camera to buy my ticket. Now I have to view the world through my eyes and not my lens. An ugly reality.

The cheques are pressed tight to my belly and making me sweat. Everyone here is a thief. They have saucer eyes and long fingers, and they babble to each other, tongues fat, lazy lizards in their mouths. I have thought of nothing but leaving for the past two days and this money is my only way out.

I am dragged from this waveless hole by a memory of how the trip began.

✳ ✳ ✳ ✳ ✳

Castro's last postcard is of a spitting reef break. Palm leaves peep from a corner and the steep profile of a mountain sneers from one side. The card is printed on cheap paper, the colours drifting from each other like badly mixed paint. It is greasy with my fingerprints. I want to pull out the borders so I can see more. Instead I turn it over for the millionth time.

> *Hey, Goog*
> *I am heading south. Meet me at the Mimpi*

Manis Guesthouse, Kupang, Timor on the 24th.
Seeya, Castro

I am on the flight to Kupang, and the plane is losing paint faster than it is gaining height. The seats are ripped, overhead lockers gape, drooling baggage on people's heads. The sky is the colour of an elephant's arse and I am way too small and easily snapped, hanging like a twig beneath it. Our dodgy propellers drone a death march as we bounce between clouds. I scour the flight mag for exits, for crash positions – bend over and kiss your arse goodbye.

I am not a bird. My bones are too heavy; they are filled with stones and seawater. I will fall like a granite angel and rocket, screaming, into the warm, dark ocean. My orange life jacket with its lame-arse whistle will go down with me. Not much of a splash.

After three centuries, we graze the tarmac, rise, dip, wallop it hard, a scream, blue smoke pours from the tyres, the wings break up – rectangles of metal angle towards the sky. The man next to me smiles madly and I want to smack him, tell him to snap out of it, to be very afraid. The plane slows and bumps over the runway towards the bright lights of a building. We are told to remain seated but everyone stands up and starts pulling their bags down. The madman beside me says, 'Good landing.' He gives it a double thumbs up. '*Bagus* this one – good. Normal one bad.'

At customs, I score a two-month visa and a greasy look

from the immigration bloke. I have eight weeks to find Castro who has been missing in Indo for a year. The sums don't add up. How has he managed to stay here for a year when everyone else only gets sixty days?

Outside, Disco Jerry – the taxi driver from hell – lifts me from the packs of shouting drivers and scam merchants. He drives like a lunatic to the Mimpi Manis, all the way telling me how bad it is.

'*Mimpi manis* mean sweet dream, ha ha. Bad dream. Nightmare!'

He drives looking at me and not at the road. His clove cigarette crackles and drops ash on my knees. He drives with his blow-up Teletubby doll – Laa-Laa – beside him in the front seat.

The Mimpi Manis turns out to be no Hilton. Sweet Dreams! Ha ha! If I could sleep I would dream, but the dreams would be of the Bee Gees' karaoke club in the lobby, of the skin-toned lizards clicking on the walls and the fat bedbugs that rattle under my sheets at lights-out.

Even eating is no fun. Everything smells of bad oil and chillies. There are beggars and shit out the front of the restaurants.

＊＊＊＊＊

'Can I have that?' a voice says, breaking into my misery. He is whippet-thin and tall as the Statue of Liberty. He sounds American.

'What?'

'That?' He points to my pile of bones and gristle, the maggots of rice clinging to the rim of the plate, the humping flies.

'Take it,' I say. 'It's yours. Bon appétit.' I *never* do French. Mum made me stick at it until year nine, but I got sick of verbs and accents, and that whole *le–la* bullshit. Plus it always sounds so wanky; I don't know how the French get away with it. But strange things happen sometimes when I speak before I think. Stuff leaks out. Of course, everyone is always way smarter in their head, but how often does it break the surface?

'Obliged,' he says and pulls a small floppy dog from the hessian sack on his shoulder. He plops it beside the table and shoves the plate of bones under its nose.

'Shouldn't feed a dog chook bones, they choke or something.' I don't know if this is true, but it seems like the right thing to say.

He just looks at me. The dog looks at the pile of bones and sniffs them. He licks the air in front of the plate but has the sense not to eat those bones. Smart dog. He cocks his leg against the table. He looks sick. Ribs showing through his raggedy coat.

The waiter stands in the puddle of dog piss. It splashes on his bare leg, but he pretends not to notice.

'*Apa?*' he says. I don't know what it means but it doesn't sound friendly.

The dog-man doesn't seem to care. He smiles at the waiter with his very white teeth. 'Water?' he asks.

The waiter points a long-nailed finger at the jug on the table, turns his back and flip-flops to the front counter. He leaves a trail of wet prints behind him, but they soon dry to nothing.

'Niagara,' says the dog-man and holds out a sweaty palm. 'Niagara Falls.'

I open my mouth to tell him my name is Goog but he shows me his flat palm.

'Yeah, I know. Kinda weird name and all, but Mom and Sir were fall freaks. Married at Niagara and spent the next twenty summers beside every cascade and cataract they could photograph. Got two brothers and one sister. Betchar'yall wondrin what they're called?'

I'm not; I'm wondering why he calls his dad 'Sir'. But I nod anyway.

'Sister's Victoria after that great fall in Africa. She's okay with her name, kinda normal. Brothers are another story.' He looks out at the darkening sky and the kero lamps dotting the street like small stars. 'Angel's the youngest. Middle brother got Krimmler after some Austrian thing.' Niagara purses his lips and lets go a wolf whistle. His dog looks up, ears cocked, ready for action. 'Krimmler! He's been pissed about that one all his life. Gonna change it when he's old enough. "Not while you're under my roof," says Sir. Old bastard.'

I leave the 'Sir' alone and ask instead, 'What's your dog's name?'

'Belacan,' answers Niagara. 'It's spelt with a C but you say it like a CH – *blaachaan*. Means prawn paste, they tell me. Bouquet on him like a dead skunk when I found him. Cleaned him up and now he goes where I go.'

'And where is that?' I ask.

'North,' he says.

'Far north?' There's not too much south of here until you hit Australia.

'All the way, man – Sumatra.' He bends down and pats Belacan on the head. 'All the freakin way.'

I touch my Lonely Planet, its spine barely crinkled. 'Me too,' I say, as if I know.

He smiles at my too-new guidebook. His tweezer-thin eyebrows shoot off at strange angles to his eyes and he twists a couple of big horns into his gelled hair.

'Keep a secret?' he asks, and moves in until I can see the dirty pores on his nose.

'Yeah, I guess so.'

He pushes in beside me and plonks his hessian sack on the table. He reaches into the sack and battles with his stuff for a while. Then he pulls out a book and slaps it in front of me.

It's just a notebook, nothing special. There is a drawing of a shadow puppet on the cover. It has a long thin nose and a laced crown rising over its head. I've seen these puppets before, in Castro's room in Torquay. The words *Jalan Jalan Indonesia 1971–1975* are written in faded black pen across the bottom of the book.

'My uncle's journal. Max Falls. He was twenty-one – same age as me – when he got sent to Vietnam.' Niagara looks down at Belacan and I struggle to stay locked in the present, struggle with my dad's memory; how *he* went to Vietnam and how he left part of himself there.

Niagara continues. 'Died in the fall of last year. Lonely old man. No wife or family and me his only friend in the world.'

Beads of sweat appear on Niagara's temples and begin the long trek round his jaw. He pours a tumbler of dirty water and takes a drink. I watch while his Adam's apple admits a couple of million water bugs into his throat. He wipes his mouth with the back of his hand.

'This was what he left me. Called it his "legacy" and wrote that I should "follow my heart and my dreams wherever they may lead". Sir missed the draft. Flat feet or tunnel vision, something like that. Married my mom and had kids. Called Uncle Max "a messed-up hypocrite", said he should settle *down* and grow *up*. But Uncle Max kept sending me cards. Two years surfing in Costa Rica, malaria and dysentery nearly finished him. Survived bombs in Beirut and dodged Vietcong bullets. Know what finally got him?'

I shake my head. I don't know this guy and I don't want this conversation. I want to return to being lonely and scared.

'It's a sad story.' Niagara raises his thin eyebrows so they look like bent paperclips. 'This British dude came to the grocery store I was working at. He said he knew my uncle – from Asia. Apparently he'd got a call that Max had choked on his own vomit. Scored a six-foot hole and a plywood box in Locust Grove, Oklahoma. No one went to his funeral.' Niagara wipes his eyes on his arm. 'The dude gave me Uncle Max's journal and a pile of dough he'd been saving for me.'

I don't know what to say. This is bigger than me. I can see this conversation leaking from Niagara's mouth, black and foul, heavy with the smell of gunpowder. I want to stuff it back in. I came here to surf and find my dead friend, not to gather someone else's troubles and carry them like a pack on my journey. I stand up to go, but Niagara grabs me by the sleeve.

I shrug off his hand but he says, 'Sorry, man. Didn't mean to heavy-you-out or anything. How bout I buy you a brewski?'

Across the road, the Mimpi Manis's neon is farting sick light into the humid night. I think of my friends: the bedbugs, the flesh-lizards and the karaoke zombies cutting sick on the Bee Gees in the lobby.

I let Niagara buy me that beer, and I make my choice. Life and travel are much the same – you get to a fork in the road and you have two ways to go. You have to make a decision. So you choose a road and you start walking. And once you do, you are fully committed to that road; you can't travel both at once. And even if you want to, you can't go back to the fork. If you do, the road will have changed or someone will have switched the signs.

So we drink beers. Warm beers with ice. Bir Bintang with the labels missing and the glass white where their bellies have rubbed together in their long journey through the islands. We drink beers until there is a platoon of bottles at attention on the table and the fluoro light in the restaurant throbs. Beetles knock against the light and drop onto our table. They fall into our beers and we drink them. We spit them onto the floor and Belacan worries them with his paw, crunches their hard black shells with his teeth. Outside, cicadas swamp the air with their high-pitched whine. And it rings in my ears and the moon gets big and Niagara and I are best mates and we make our plans right there to travel together. To follow Uncle Max's diary and to find Castro.

'Is he Cuban?' Niagara asks.

'No, we called him that because his last name was Fidle. Sort of like Fidel. It seemed funny at the time.'

'How come he took off with no goodbyes?'

'We were surfing. He'd gone in bleeding and the water ended up full of his broken board. I was sure he got taken by a shark. But then something funny happened.'

'Funny ha-ha or funny weird?' asks Niagara.

'Weird. Definitely.'

My mind drifts back to the German tourists we met on the Great Ocean Road. Castro, Aldo and I were still together. The next time I saw the Germans was at Margaret River, and I was alone – Castro had disappeared in the Bight, then Aldo was kidnapped by Jasper while I was out surfing. The Germans told me they had passed someone hitching on the desert road near where Castro disappeared; someone hitching in a wetsuit. That made me doubt his death. That and the postcards.

I grab a bundle from my pack. It is wrapped in a bandana Mum sent me at Custard Sam's; one of Dad's she found while clearing out his stuff. Inside the bundle is a stack of postcards. I fan them like a poker deck over the table.

'I started getting these after Castro went missing.' There are eleven pictures of the most gnarly, awesome breaks I have ever seen – peaks, thick wedges, peeling lefts and rights.

Niagara flips them over one by one. They begin with *Hey, Goog* and end *Seeya, Castro*. In between he bangs on about how good the waves are and that I should be there cutting sick with him.

'No captions,' says Niagara. 'And he doesn't say where he is. How the hell are you going to trace him?'

'Beats me. He never mentions any towns or names the breaks.' I pull one more card from my pocket. 'This one's from Uluwatu – *Ulus* – the only break I know one hundred per cent. Castro's all-time favourite. This was the first card I got, just after he disappeared.'

But this is the one I don't trust. That's why I don't keep it with the others. I don't let on to Niagara that it might not have been Castro who sent it. That would mean explaining Jasper.

Niagara grabs the card. 'There's no message on this one. How do you even know it was from him?'

'It was sent to the same address as all the others – Custard Sam's Backpackers, Margaret River. The envelope had Castro's writing on it.' But even saying it out loud doesn't make it true.

'Was there anything else in the envelope?'

'Just some page of a book that Castro was reading before he vanished.'

'That could be a clue.'

The street goes quiet. The cicadas take a rest.

'I lost it,' I say.

'You what?'

'It was just one page with a stupid quote underlined. Something about overcoming fear and being curious and learning stuff.'

'Probably meant diddly-squat.' He swills the dregs of his beer and stares at them like he is reading tea-leaves. 'So what are you going to do now?'

'I'm going to drink beer,' I say, draining my glass.

'*Dua* Bintang!' shouts Niagara, and the waiter brings two more beers and we pour them over the rough-cut lumps of ice and toast our one road split into two. And I blink and try to focus on just how we are going to do this – travel two roads at once – but the night is hot and endless and there is plenty of time to worry about it tomorrow.

I have never experienced a hangover in the tropics. It is not good. My brain has welded itself to the inside of my skull and it hurts like hell. Light screams through the barred window of my room. The smell of burnt plastic and boiled eggs claws its way up from the lobby. I can hear the Gibb brothers belting out *Staying Alive*.

I fall out of bed and crawl to the door. Reaching up, I open it and stumble to the landing. In the lobby, the karaoke zombies are at it already, following the bouncing white dot on the TV and singing along. The Bee Gees are singing about how they are walking and how they are good with the ladies and how they are managing to stay alive.

And the zombies are undead. Like Castro.

If I puked right now, I could hit them all. They are sitting like monkeys on the cane lounge with a build-up of coffee cups, Fanta bottles and cigarette butts around them.

I crawl back to my room, switch on the fan, collapse on the bed and run my fingertips over the bedbug welts on my chest and legs. The fan swings long loops of cobweb at the wall. I try to think, but my brain hurts so much that I stop before I break something. I meditate on the fan. It rocks and makes me feel sick. It would chop me in two if it fell. I turn it off, go into the bathroom and pour a bucket of water over me. It is like a punch in the head – cold and complete. The bathroom walls throb like my pulse as I stagger around. I finally find the door and drop onto my bed.

My board is propped in the corner. That board crossed 'The Paddock' with me, all the way from Torquay to Margaret River to here. Mum bought it before I left. My not-quite-rhino-chaser – I surfed huge *Elephants* with it, and pissy little *Margarets* on the night we arrived. The board I paddled into the Bight the day Castro disappeared. A groan gurgles up from inside me and I cover my head with the pillow. I bite it hard and it tastes like anchovies.

There is a knock at the door.

'Gurg?' It's Niagara.

I lie completely still with the pillow over my head.

'Gurg? Y'in there?'

'No. And the name's Goog. There's two o's in it,' I croak.

'Come on, Gurg, let Niagara in. The Bee Gees are killing me.'

I unlock the door then fall on the bed and cover my head with the anchovy pillow.

'Hey, Gurg. It's a beautiful day, let's get some food. Walk around. See what we can see.'

'Piss off.'

'Hey, don't be like that, dude.'

'Piss off!' Why won't this drop kick leave me alone?

'Okay, okay, I can take a hint. Niagara knows when he's not wanted. I'm outta here.' The door closes and I can hear the clopping of feet down the landing.

I hold my breath and listen. The Bee Gees are warbling *Tragedy* and the karaoke zombies are heavy on top of it. I listen and everything else is quiet. A motorbike wasps along our narrow street. Niagara goes. He actually buggers off. I feel tiny needles of guilt stabbing me. Sometimes I can be a bit on the harsh side.

'Gurg.' It's Niagara's muffled voice at the door. 'I was

going to go, and I did, but then I thought you probably *did* want company but you were just too shy to admit it and it's no good eating breakfast alone and we are almost blood brothers—'

I open the door. He's wearing a huge Canadian-flag shirt with the words GO ON ASK ME across the chest. I want to ask him what is all this shit about blood brothers but the shirt changes my foggy mind.

'You're Canadian?'

'Hell no.'

'What's with the shirt then?'

He leans on the doorjamb like he's the cleverest man alive and says, 'Deflects unfriendly fire.'

'Mate, do you always talk like you swallowed a book of riddles?'

'A lot of people don't like Americans.'

'Well, do you blame them?' I say and his tweezerbrows drop low over his eyes. 'I mean you guys can't make a movie like *Point Break* and expect to get away with it.'

He laughs a too big laugh. 'Yeah, but what about *Big Wednesday*.'

'Classic!' I admit.

'*Endless Summer One* and *Two*.'

'*One* is classic. *Two* will be in about twenty years.'

'I gotta agree with you about *Point Break* though. Bigtime crapola.'

'Shithouse!'

'Shithouse,' he says. 'Wanna get some breakfast? I know a good place for noodles.'

I look at my watch – 7.15am. Noodles?

'Okay,' I say. 'I'll just drag some shorts on.'

'So you've read it then?' I ask over a bowl of thick egg-noodles – good hangover food, spicy and hot.

Niagara schloops a noodle into his mouth. 'The journal?'

I nod.

'The first page brought me here. I'm only going to read it as I travel it, that's what Uncle Max wanted. "Don't get ahead of yourself," he wrote. "Live in the now."'

Niagara fishes the book from his sack and puts it on the table. I notice the shadow puppet on the cover. 'What's with this?' I ask.

'It's a shadow puppet.'

'Yeah, I know that much.' Castro was always showing them to me.

'*Wayang kulit.* Or as I like to say, *why-man, cool-it!*' He shoots me the hang loose sign, pure wankfish. 'Uncle Max was a *dalang* – a puppet master – did a lot of training in Java. The stories came across here from India. All gods and heroes and talking monkeys – crazy-ass shit. Before TV, village kids had *wayang kulit.*'

'I'll stick with TV,' I say.

'Uncle Max could do magic with those puppets. They're just a scrap of leather on a stick but, boy, could he make them mothers come alive. Make you lose touch with reality.'

Not for me, I think as I stare into the reality of my noodles, at the watery soup and thin strips of goat meat. Belacan licks my hand.

'What's with the dog, Niagara?'

He reaches down and worries a blob of chewing gum on Belacan's coat as he answers. 'My uncle had a pooch in Indonesia. Called it Nix after the president that packed him off to Nam. I had to get one as well. It's all part of the trip.'

Everything boomerangs to Uncle Max. Niagara is obsessed.

He looks up from Belacan at me. 'So what about Castro?' he asks.

'Well, he said to meet him at the Mimpi Manis on the 24th. Today's the 27th and nothing.'

'What about the card with the name on it – Oloomawatoo?'

I try to think of an explanation that doesn't involve Jasper and the dark thoughts that surround him. 'Uluwatu's in Bali. Miles away. Plus it's over a year ago. He'd be long gone by now.'

'Looks like your trail's gone cold,' Niagara says as he picks a noodle off his chin.

'Dunno what to do next. Castro was supposed to be here. But he's also supposed to be dead.' I push at my temples, my brain hurts.

The sun is cooking the pavement in front of the noodle stall and spearing us through our shabby umbrella. I can smell tar bubbling on the road.

'So you may's well come with me. Maybe you'll pick up the trail later. He must be heading north; everyone goes north from here.'

We talked about this last night, I think. But today it makes no sense.

'*Everyone* goes north,' Niagara repeats and raises his thin eyebrows.

'Sumatra?'

'Well, yeah, Sumatra. Bout as far north as you can get. That's where Uncle Max ended up. Sir told me he lived in some malaria camp on Pulau Nias. He loved to surf. Born on the Californian coast, see. Salt water in his blood.'

'Castro would hit every surf spot he could,' I said. 'So I suppose travelling together could work. I mean if we are heading in the same direction.'

I don't let on about how this place scares the shit out of me. How it seems better when there's someone to share it with. I could head to Sumba or Pulau Roti, check out the waves, ask about Castro. But I would have to do it on my own and I just don't think I'd make it.

'That settles it, man. We go together, watch out for each other. Blood brothers, remember.'

I don't remember, but I don't have a better plan, short of returning to Torquay, or to Margaret River for another season at Custard Sam's. Another year of making beds and cleaning other people's pubes from shower drains. I don't think so.

'So, where to first?'

Niagara puts down his fork and opens the journal.

29 June 1971

Pulau Lembata

Herman Melville couldn't have written this place sweeter if he'd imagined Moby Dick *in the Savu Sea. The towns of Nantucket have nothing on Lamalera. Here the natives beat out to sea at the first sign of a whale fluke.* Baleo! Baleo! *they cry and roll their heavy wooden boats down the beach. They pull over the shorebreak and paddle for the horizon. They are strong and brave and full of fear and respect. They raise their woven palm sails and the wind shovels them toward Timor.*

THE HARPOON MAN

i shake hands with the man
who rides the backs of whales
who sharpens steel
and leaps from the bow of the boat

his sea is full of danger
of dark shapes that move
beneath the hull

his sea is the provider
and the taker of life
it is the deceiver

on days
when whales trawl up the coast
everyone has one eye on the water

the whale's back is broad
its tail can take a life

up there in the bow
he waits . . .

I am not into poetry. My ex-girlfriend, Marcella, was and it bored the shit out of me. *Prithy* this and *doth* that. But Uncle Max had me with the harpoon man. And I am not into harpooning whales. My mum has whale recordings slotted in among her Deep Purple and Hendrix.

My Lonely Planet suddenly doesn't seem enough. It feels right to follow a dead man's words through the sea-snake spine of islands. To use a dead man's words until I find the right path to *my* dead friend.

3 Whale watching

Lamalera, Lembata

'Hello, misterrr!'

The boy is made from snot and mud and snarled black hair. He is about ten years old and his T-shirt says FOETUS CLASSICAL EUROPE GUESS. It is four sizes too big, ripped at the armpits. His teeth are like bathroom tiles – huge, white, square, chipped on the bottom corners as if he has often opened bottle caps with them.

My brain is in low gear after our trip – fourteen hours on a ferry, a four-hour shake-up in a rusting truck-bus and an hour's slog with board, backpack and Niagara's endless bullshit, down a sun-baked dirt road to this whalebone village. I am hungry for food and surf but the water is crap – flat as a freeway cat and dull like old silver.

'Hello,' I say and hold up my flat palm – a peace-giving injun in an old Western movie.

'Hello, misterrr,' he says again.

He has a stick and a small wheel of rubber cut from the tread of a tyre. There is a river of green running from his nose and over his top lip. He stands in a doorway arched with long jawbones. The town snakes in two untidy rows between the hills and the beach. Stone walls are gapped with mud; green and blue shutters are flapped open. Plants grow from giant spine bones. This is not a whale-friendly town.

'Hello, misterrr.'

'Hello, buddy,' says Niagara, kneeling down to the boy's level. Niagara's hair is particularly scary this morning. His eyebrows are hairline fractures on his forehead.

The boy looks at him out of the corners of his eyes. They narrow and he opens his mouth and fires. 'Hellomisterrr . . . hellomisterrr . . . hellomisterrr . . . hellomisterrr . . . hellomisterrr . . . hellomisterrr . . . hellomisterrr . . . hellomisterrr . . . hellomisterrr . . .'

I grab Niagara by the strap of his pack and we back away. The kid follows.

'Hellomisterrr . . . hellomisterrr . . . hellomisterrr . . . hellomisterrr . . . hellomisterrr . . . hellomisterrr . . . hellomisterrr . . .' He keeps coming.

This kid is pissing me off. I want to snatch him by his skinny shoulders and shake him but his mother is watching from the doorway now and she looks happy and proud. Other kids pop their heads out of windows and doors. They rush out onto the street. Their mothers look at them lovingly as they

chant, 'Hellomisterrr . . . hellomisterrr . . . hellomisterrr . . .'
They are a green-nosed and torn-clothed posse, but they are
lively little buggers.

Then one kid struts onto the street and holds his hand up
for silence. He puffs out his chest and points at us. He smiles
and opens his mouth. 'Mista Lubbalubba,' he says. 'Mista
Bombastic.' I remember the hit song of the nineties, the one
with those lyrics. The pseudo-rap rasta Shaggy bigging it up.
Mister Bombastic – his hit on high rotation all through the
summer in Torquay. Somehow it must have made it here and
stuck.

Suddenly, the whole crew explodes in a machine-gun
rattle of chants. 'Mistalubbalubba . . . mistalubbalubba . . .
mistalubbalubba . . . mistabombastic . . . mistabombastic . . .
hellomisterrr . . . hellomisterrr . . . mistalubbalubba . . . hellomisterrr . . . hellomisterrr . . .'

We run through the town with our tail of chanting kids
and smiling mothers. What kind of Shaggy-worshipping,
whale-butchering town is this?

The sun is angry as we take the far hill to upper Lamalera.
My board clanks against my legs and the straps of my pack
bite deep into my shoulders. It's hard going. The road is
uneven, cobbled with rough stone blocks, and the hot air
is too thick to breathe.

Eventually, the kids give up. They stand for a while
shadow-boxing and doing handstands. Then they run down
the hill, rolling bike tyres and their small rubber wheels ahead

of them with sticks and still chanting, 'Mistalubbalubba . . . mistalubbalubba . . .'

Stopping to catch our breath, we look down on the bay with its circle of thatched boathouses. The water, though surfless, looks inviting. But then Niagara points out a red flower of blood on a rock and a huge backbone slopping in the shorebreak. There are black-haired pigs cleaning up flecks of snowy fat from the volcanic sand.

Behind us are racks filled with drying strips of meat, oil dripping down corrugated iron gutters and into tins. The slabs of meat are dark red, turning to black, with seams of fat marbled through them. The air is big with the smell of whale meat. It slips, like oiled rubber, into our throats and noses. In the middle of these racks stands a small man. He calls us with his hand facing downwards like he is paddling an invisible board. A Dutch guy on the boat from Timor told us he would be here. He said he is always watching the water, waiting for strangers to arrive. The small man turns and we follow him up a path through the maze of drying racks and drip trays.

Vitalis Homestay is two rooms. It is the best hotel in town, according to the Dutch guy. One room is ours, crammed with two rickety bunk beds, a patchy mirror on one wall. The other is the dining room with a plastic covered table and whale-oil lamps. The tiny cupboard that holds Vitalis's bed runs off the dining room and the kitchen is outside. Through the window is a view over the whole village – iron roofs rusting in the salt-heavy air.

We are sitting at the table, studying Niagara's map. I run my finger up the long chain of islands that make up Indonesia. I see shapes in these islands, like cloud reflections in a mirrored sea. Flores is a whale, its tail raising the islands of Lembata, Solor and Adonara. Above, Sulawesi is an angelfish swimming to the reef of Kalimantan. Sumbawa is a frog pushing a wheelbarrow. Lombok is a jellyfish; Bali, a trained dog balancing on the ball of the Bukit Peninsula. Java is a hungry seal. Finally, the furthest island and the biggest – Sumatra. Here, I see nothing. I have heard too much about this place from other people to make it mine. The legendary surf-islands of Nias and the Mentawais. The possibilities of pinprick atolls and a huge angry ocean. Sumatra has no shape I can recognise. Not yet.

Vitalis's wife, Marina, brings us dinner. Black lumps with rice and two-minute noodles. Niagara heaps his plate high and tucks in. I am slower. There is something strange about these black things – they look cancerous. I bring a piece to my nose and it smells oily and wrong. I poke my tongue at it; it tastes like the eraser at the end of a pencil. I put it in my mouth, grip the fork with my teeth and drag it onto my tongue. It sits like a toad, heavy and poisonous, waiting for me to make the next move. I shift it to my back teeth and give it a slow grind. It breaks up into something that is not quite fish and not quite meat. It is gritty and fatty and horrible. I look at Niagara and he is smiling and chewing and piling more black shit onto his plate.

Vitalis comes in and says, '*Ikan paus.*'

'What?' I am looking for somewhere to spit my mouthful of cancerous mush.

'*Ikan paus*,' says Vitalis. 'Whale.'

Now I feel sick, really sick. I'm not a new-agey, dolphiny, dreamcatchery kind of guy but *eating* whales is pushing me too far. Marina comes to the door and asks him a question and when he turns away, I quietly drop my whale-meat into my hand and place it gently under the table by Belacan's paws. He sniffs it and looks up at me with his sad brown eyes. I clean my mouth out with some instant noodles and rice.

Vitalis's body is cranked with age, his face a contour map with ridges and valleys chiselled deep into his dark brown skin. It is getting dark outside and he puts a match to the whale oil in the shallow tin dish on the table. It catches and sends an orange glow around the room – to his shelf of battered books and the harpoon heads on the wall.

'Ancestors,' he says with the light dancing across his face. 'Come here on back of Blue Whale. This one we do not hunt. Manta ray, dolphin, shark, we hunt. The whale keep us alive, we use him all. Bone, oil, blubber, meat – we share between the clan that catches.' He turns over our map and pulls a pen from a drawer. Sketching the outline of a whale, he divides it up into cuts like a butcher's poster. Pointing to the area around the fin and then the nose of the whale, he says, 'These for harpooner. This,' he stabs a small rectangle below the fin, 'for harpoon-maker. The eye bit for first clan of Lamalera. Below tail for boss of clan that killed whale.'

Soon the whole whale is divided between the village – the boatbuilders, their family, those who help haul the boat up the beach. This huge animal is reduced to strips drying in the sun, to oil and blubber and a curving set of bones. I don't know what to feel. I have seen films of Japanese boats exploding harpoons at whales, dragging them into the gaping mouths of factory ships. It's easy to be annoyed at that.

'Long ago,' says Vitalis, 'one crew towed too very far out by whale. He die and they tow him to island near Pantar. Cut whale and dry. Sail home. Village make ceremony for death of crew already. When crew walk into village, village think they is ghost. Ghost walking.' Vitalis smiles and shakes his head. 'Crew say, no, this me, this my sarong, my knife, my body. I am not ghost.' The whale-oil lamp spits a small flare into the air. 'Hunting whale is danger. Very danger.'

Niagara opens his uncle's diary and reads.

20 July 1971

Lamalera, Lembata

Whale hunt this morning. I heard the call and saw the logs dropped on the beach, ready for the launching of the boats. The flukes were rising out toward the horizon, maybe four or five whales. When I got to the beach, the men were already shoving the boat into the shorebreak. I could feel my gut tighten, that terrible fear that I thought only existed in the scrub and rice fields of Nam, those places of little cover where anything can happen. I knew this time I would have to beat it, to meet it head on, so I grabbed the gunwale of the nearest boat and helped push her to the water. Beyond the surf, with our palm sail raised –

Niagara shuts the book and Vitalis and I look up, surprised.

'Don't wanna get ahead of ourselves, do we, Gurg?' he says.

It is morning and I have been awake all night with mosquitoes and snoring. My mosssie net has a hole in it the size and shape of Java, and through it I can see the Savu Sea, calm and glittering in the early light. Niagara is on his back in the bunk opposite. His mouth is open and his bottom lip is trembling as he snores. Around him is everything I own. I have thrown all my gear at him in the hope that he would shut up. Belacan is sharing his pillow and he is whimpering in his sleep as if he is chasing rats. They make a lovely couple.

Then, over the snoring, I hear a call from the beach. *'Baleo! Baleo!'* It is quiet for a moment and then another call. *'Baleo! Baleo!'* I push myself onto my elbows. Down on the beach, there are sets of logs running from three of the boathouses to the surf. The crews are nosing their boats towards the water.

'Niagara!' I shout. He rolls over to the wall. I jump out of bed and grab his shoulder. He turns to me, pig-ugly, his gelled hair flat against his head and crumbed with sand, his eyes swollen with sleep.

'Come on, man!' I say. 'We gotta go. The boats are sailing.'

'Wha?' he says, tongue a sea cucumber in his mouth.

'Whaleboats, Niags. They're going out.'

'I thought you didn't want to. You said last night.'

I did. He's right. 'I did,' I say, 'And I don't. But *you* do. And I want to watch you kill yourself.'

'What a guy,' says Niagara and pulls on a pair of fluoro yellow shorts and a T-shirt that shouts I'M AUSSIE, YES I AM! He's taking this whole undercover American thing way too far.

The sand is already hot. I count eight or nine boats out at sea, sails up and beating for the horizon. Another is struggling with the shorebreak. Finally it breaks through and, as we get to the water's edge, the crew paddle beyond the two-foot waves and raise a holey sail on an A-frame mast.

'Shit,' says Niagara. 'Shit and godammit.' His bloodshot eyes are willing the boats back but they are long gone.

We stroll up to the boathouses where a lazy crew is sharpening knives, mending nets and smoking roll-your-own palm leaves.

'You cowboys going out?' says Niagara, pointing to the sea. I am sure he won't be understood but an old man with a base-ball cap and a blue sarong says, '*Tidak*.' And shakes his head.

'Rupiah,' says Niagara and fans a wad of ten-thousands in front of them.

The man in the cap looks at the money and then at the sea. He rubs his smooth brown belly and yawns. Shrugging, he grabs the cash and shouts his crew onto their feet.

We roll the boat down the beach on logs. They are lumpy and twisted like Mallee fence posts. The boat is full of wormholes but heavy as lead. It doesn't roll well. This boathouse is the furthest from the sea and on the steepest part of the beach. This clan got the leftovers when real estate was being handed out. The steepness of the beach works in our favour, though, and soon the boat is nose first in the shorebreak. I bend down, grab Belacan and step away. The crew stops and looks at me.

Niagara says, 'Whatcher doing, dude?'

'I'm not going, Niags.'

'Come on, man,' he says.

'Who'll look after Belacan?'

'Leave him with the kids. He'll be fine.'

'They eat dogs round here.'

'They eat whales around here, Gurg!' he says and, grabbing Belacan, hands him to one of the Hellomisterrr Brigade from yesterday.

'I don't want to go, Niagara. This whale hunting business was your idea. It's between you and your uncle. I'm looking for Castro and I'm pretty sure I'm not going to find him in the belly of a whale.' I don't say anything about the belly of a shark, but I think it.

'Gurg, this is the chance of a lifetime.'

I hate this. I can feel the pressure building like a too-full balloon. Everyone's eyes are on me. Mr Lubbalubba and the Hellomisterrr Brigade are watching as if to say, 'Even *we* would go if we were allowed, and we're only kids.' But I really don't want to get in that boat. It's not just the danger and not just the hunting-killing thing; it's both of them roped together.

We are standing on this volcanic sand beach with the sun burning holes in us and we are stalemated. The crew is watching, taking long drags on their palm leaf smokes and squinting at us. I can feel the soles of my feet getting hotter and hotter. The water seems so close. But if I step towards it, it will seem like I am giving in, like I am going to hop on that clunky wooden boat and head out for a spot of whale hunting. No way.

But the black sand is hot. Too hot. It has pulled all the fire from the sun and held it just so it can blister my feet. The water is calling – shoosh-shoosh-shoosh – and my feet are searing. The kids are wearing thin rubber thongs, broken plastic sandals. They know not to step on this beach without protection.

Suddenly I can't take it anymore. I run to the sea and stand with my ankles in the cool water. The crew push the boat forward and the man with the cap and the blue sarong shoves me roughly on board and we are paddling through the shorey and I know what those drinkers in ancient pubs must have felt like when they woke up the next morning on a ship bound for Australia or America or the edge of the world. Niagara is grinning like a halfwit. The bastard.

The men raise the twin poles of our mast and hoist our sail. It has more holes in it than a wino's singlet. The hull is as gappy as an old fence and stuffed with newspaper and tar. A young guy bales continually with a bamboo scoop but I don't think he will be able to keep it up for long. The ocean is hungry for this boat. It wants it bad.

In the stern, an old bloke in a faded pink hat steers. His arms are kelp stems – taut, dark and smooth. He accepts a cup of water poured from a pottery urn. The man who hands it to him offers me a cup, too, but I just look at it like it's the most dangerous thing about this trip. Mum told me three things before I left: don't drink the water, don't get into trouble and don't forget the way home.

We are trying to catch the other boats but they have a good start on us. They are chasing the whales on their westward run up the coast and we are chasing their wakes. Suddenly, one of the boats up ahead drops its sail. There is a rattle of excitement onboard and our crew tweaks our rigging and we pick up speed. But we are still too far away. Just as it seems like we are getting closer, the other boat moves. Its sail is still down but it is getting further from us. Our harpoon man shouts from the bow and points. There is a dark stain on the sea.

It is blood, lots of it, and it is tumbling into the depths like an upturned explosion. Fish are flashing through it. Barracuda, sleek and deadly as missiles. Tiny arrowheads of light, a shoal of bait-fish rippling like a chain mail coat. Then I notice a big triangle of fin, curving, dark – a memory of hell.

We drop our sail and the harpoon man selects a bamboo pole and slots a steel head into it. The harpoon head is curved like the fork of a tree, beaten flat and sharp along one edge. Clambering to the bow of the boat, he climbs out on the ladder-shaped prow. He stands there for a moment, balanced like a heron, waiting. When the dark back of the shark appears and the tip of its fin slices the surface of the water, the harpoon man jumps up and out of the boat, lunging at it.

The water is whipped white, then red as the shark thrashes. The harpoon has gone deep. Dark blood gushes from the shark and into the sea. Rope whips over the worn gunnel and into the water. The shark is diving and the crew shrinks away from the deadly coils unravelling like a tornado on the deck.

The harpoon man is swimming frantically towards the boat but the rope has been tied off and we are being towed away by the shark.

Another fin appears, then another, until our patch of ocean is infested with sharks, their tails beating the water, blood rushing through their gills. The harpoon man is right amongst it, his eyes crazy with fear. He is pulling huge scoops of red water with his hands. He is swimming in blood.

Big eel-like memories come winding up from inside me. And then it is Castro in that water and I am frozen, open-mouthed, watching as the huge, greedy shark raises the water behind him. My mouth is dry. I turn to the crew but they are frozen too.

I am ready to jump in the water but the harpoon man's knuckles suddenly appear on the smooth gunnels of the boat. The mop of his hair is just visible, knotted with seawater and strings of blood. He is too tired to pull himself in. Reaching under his arms, I drag him up and over the side. He lies there smiling and dripping pink water. It soaks into my bare soles.

The shark tires quickly and the crew hauls on the stiff rope that links it to us. They pull until it is beside the boat, until we can see the beast's cold grey eye and the black crescents of its gill slits. The harpooner thrusts another sharpened head into its back and, as the bamboo pole breaks off, he grabs the line. There is no way the shark is getting free now. It shudders and thumps against the boat and I am sickened by its pain.

And slowly the shark dies and its eye goes dull and the sea gently turns its fins. I feel like crying, but I know these men would never understand. I am not even sure that I do. I used to dream of revenge, of killing every last one of the bastards from Torquay to Margaret River until I got the one that killed Castro. Not now.

Then the shark's body jerks and for a moment it has come back to life. It jerks again and I peer down into the water and spot another shark shoving its blunt snout deep into the corpse's side.

Dad once told me how several sharks are born alive inside their mother. They are not like other fish. They battle it out in the dark of their mother's belly, small teeth ripping, living off each other, killing the weakest and growing stronger until only one remains. If that's how they start life, it is no wonder they end up like this.

It is a long way to shore, towing our dead shark and beating off live ones with paddles and harpoon shafts. They keep coming. Each time they hit, the boat shudders and groans, and I picture its rough planks peeling apart and us falling into the dangerous sea.

In far off islands they worship these fish. Some say they are the spirits of dead people. Ghosts forever roaming the seas.

This one is mangled, torn beyond repair. But I look for hope in its dulled eyes. I look for signs of Castro.

When we hit the shorebreak, I leap off without even turning to the shark, or what remains of it. The Hellomisterr Brigade is waiting with plastic sandals, hoops, sticks and our dog. I grab Belacan and walk quickly up the beach.

One of the kids is standing on a boulder at the far corner of the bay, harpooning the sand with his thin bamboo cane, practising for the day when he can leap from the ladder-shaped prow.

'Hey, Gurg!' Niagara shouts after me. 'Are'ncha gonna help?' But I leave him and the crew to roll the heavy boat up the steepest part of the beach.

'I met him, yes.' Vitalis is studying a photo of Uncle Max. I have no photo of Castro.

'Long time before. Maybe I am fifteen, maybe I am sixteen. He had much . . . we say, *kesayuan*. I don't know English word.'

Niagara opens his pocket dictionary. '*Kesayuan*: melancholy, sadness.'

'Sadness. Much sadness. I was only a boy then but he was good man. I remember this. This and his sadness.'

'It was the war,' says Niagara. 'He had the medals but they never made up for everything else.'

I want to tell him about my dad. This would be the perfect time, but something stops me, something big sitting on my chest and squeezing the air from me. Instead I ask Vitalis, 'Have you had a guest here recently? Someone called Castro.'

'Castro?' He scratches his eyebrows. 'No. No Castro. No one for many weeks. Quiet. Too many tourists want Bali, Lombok, surfing Sumbawa. No one want Lembata.'

Me neither, I think. Why would Castro come here, anyway? To the south is Sumba – a wild island, full to bursting with gnarly reef breaks. Why would he come to this place? But Sumba has crazy tribes who will cut you up as soon as look at you and Niags won't come with me. So I'll keep tagging along with him on his loopy trek to shit-knows-where. There is safety in numbers.

I go outside with my bundle of postcards. I place them one by one on the dusty earth. They shine at me, dog-ears pricked to the birdsong afternoon. I know their backs are swarming with the wild loops of Castro's writing. Blu-tac circles oil the corners from when I stuck them to my wall in Margaret River. Every one of these cards is a place I do not know. Each one a key without a door.

I twist Dad's bandana over in my hand. It is khaki with tiny skull-and-crossbones along its borders. Mum said it was from Vietnam. It brought him luck over there.

Flattening it on the dirt, I stack my postcards neatly on top. I wrap Castro's journey in my Dad's old talisman – a symbol of his safe passage back from war.

Down at the beach, they are carving up a whale. Women are winding up the hill, the pots on their heads slopping over with meat. If I still had my camera, I would have wasted three rolls of film on this scene. Without it, I wish I could hit the sea and paddle out forever. But I am bound to this dusty road Niagara and I have split into two.

4 Black magic woman

Bajawa, Flores

Darkness is always a worry. It is bigger than me or Niagara, or this whole shitcake village. These guys could be taught a thing or two about lighting.

Our bus has died of some long-term and horrible thing and it looks like we are spending the night. There is no way I want to curl up in chook shit and vomit and wait for sunrise to curdle over the tin roofs. This place looks like a movie set – the one where a bus breaks down and the villagers creep out under the cover of dark and chop the passengers into bits and serve them up with their morning noodles. I am bent stupid by this bus and its torn seats and rice sacks. I need somewhere to stretch; somewhere safe with a forty-watt bulb and a door to lock ourselves behind.

It has been a long day. Or has it been two? I traded my

watch at lunchtime for a bunch of overripe bananas. It was a decent swap. Besides, my wallet was stuffed down low in my pack which in turn had a sack of cloves nailing it to the floor like a WWF wrestler. Time meant nothing anyway, stretching in and out like an elastic band. Snapping in our faces with its odd hours and drooping sunsets.

*****

We board in Maumere, on a beachside chocked with earthquaked houses. And then our maniac driver chain-smokes kretek and twists his battered wreck through the Florenese hills. We pick up passengers in each village along the way – women with sacks of coffee and rice, men with bicycles and black pigs. The back of the bus is hung with chickens, their legs knotted in bunches, beaks dripping onto the road. I sit for two hours holding a goat on my knee.

Everyone is sick except Niagara, the driver and me. They call out, 'Plastik!' through cupped hands and a bag is ripped from the handrail and passed back. There is a trail of vommy-filled sacks leading to Maumere.

In villages, kids batter the windows with bags of prawn crackers and peanuts before jumping inside to hassle and bargain. Near the coast they hold up wire rings of small fish, like clusters of keys, as we pass. My feet roll over red onions. I buy a boiled egg that is as green as old copper inside. I eat it and hold my nose against the tide of spew.

We keep on as if we are going to drive forever. The seat

burns my arse and rubs smooth patches into my shorts. I shiver into the cool evening.

The whole island of Flores is a waste of space. Sumba and Timor shelter it from any decent swell that would otherwise make it through the Savu Sea. Sumbawa holds the only wave potential and, to reach it, this no-mans-land of tricky mountains and dusty towns must be crossed.

On dark, there is a horrible shearing noise like something wrenching loose inside the motor. The dog-shit smell of gear oil rolls up from under the floor. The bus shudders and stops. The oldest animal in the jungle finally reaching its graveyard.

We sit still, not knowing what else to do. The driver shouts and smacks the windscreen. The lady beside me tuts quietly.

We are towed into Bajawa by a banana truck.

* * * * *

'Gurg, I ain't leaving this bus and that's that.' Niagara is hunched against the window and peering into Uncle Max's diary. Belacan is eyeing the circling packs of dogs outside the window.

I can't believe this guy. He is a bloody joke. 'This is bull-shit, Niags, and you know it! There is no way I'm spending the night cramped-up like some kind of yoga freak just to set off again in the morning. Let's get ourselves a decent night's kip and get back fresh for the road tomorrow.'

'Look, Gurg, Uncle Max didn't stop here.' He holds up the journal but I can't read it in the gloom. 'There is nothing about Bajawa. It wasn't part of his trip and so it's not going to be part of mine.'

I try to reason with him. 'If we stay here the night we're going to wake up in ice baths, minus our kidneys, passports and traveller's cheques. Why worry about Uncle Max? It's not as if he's going to complain.'

Niagara leans his forehead against the cool glass of the window. Belacan licks his hand.

'Come on, Niags, let's get out and have a poke around. If we don't discover anything we'll come right back and spend the night on the bus. If Uncle Max had been stranded here that's what he would have done. The man was up for anything.'

Niagara turns, I can see by the soft corners of his mouth I have him hooked. He says, 'This is going to end badly.'

'It'll be fine. We'll just have a quick squiz and then back on the bus. I swear.' I raise my right hand, fully ready to take an oath.

Niagara scoops up Belacan and his sack and heads for the door. I follow him before he has a chance to change his mind.

We exit to a pack of twenty mangy dogs. The driver shuts and locks the door behind us.

There is rabies here and I bet at least nineteen of these pooches have it. Their snouts are in the air, getting nosefuls of Belacan and stale vomit from our trip. Belacan lets out a pathetic, high-pitched growl, halfway between anger and fear. Niagara tightens his grip.

'Nice doggies,' he says. But he lies, because they are

twenty of the nastiest *doggies* I have ever seen. Twenty scab-backed, drippy-arsed, ring-tailed mongrels. Thirty-nine weepy-eyes. Seventy-nine crooked legs, ripped dew-claws, cracked pads, nearly every one limping. But they all look ready for a brawl.

'Nice doggies.'

My Lonely Planet is on the bus, but I remember something in it about rabies. Something about death or a series of painful shots. Something about dogs and monkeys and saliva. These dogs have plenty of saliva. It is hanging in great strings from their teeth and tongues. We are in trouble here.

'Nice, nice doggies. Good doggies.'

Just a quick squiz and then back on the bus. It must be time for the second part of the plan. I turn to signal the driver to let us in, but I can see he has his feet on the steering wheel and his beanie pulled down over his eyes. He is listening to some sad boyband tape at full kick. If it is a choice between Westlife and twenty rabid dogs it is probably safer to take our chances with the mutts.

Niagara shoots me a 'should've listened to Uncle Max' look. I put my hand on the door handle and rattle it. The biggest dog in the pack gives a low throaty growl. It rumbles down deep in my stomach, the place where fear slips loose and ends up in puddles in your boots. This dog is huge. It is brindle – the colour of bad dogs. It has one brown eye and one that looks like a shattered egg. It is me and this dog; the rest of the world shrinks to nothing. He is eyeing me, sizing up my windpipe for a decent death grip. I clench my fists as tight as I can. They are like rocks. I can feel my skin, drum-tight over my knuckles. Any tighter and they will pop through. If I can get a decent punch to the dog's scarred head then I may be in with a chance, otherwise I am rooted. My heart is playing bass guitar in my chest – something heavy from the Doors. The dog's good eye twitches. My throat closes over.

The muscles in his legs tense. He rocks back. His front legs extend and his shoulders flex out. He shoots a warning growl that raises a ridge of hair along his spine. But I am locked to his eyes.

He is in the air; in the space that kept us apart. I pull my head low to my chest to protect my throat. I bring my hands up to my face. They are way too soft, my nails like brittle shells.

His front paws hit my chest. A fleck of drool lashes my cheek like a bluebottle sting. I land hard on the dirt, my head hitting last and bouncing so I bite a chunk from my tongue. Blood fills my mouth; the taste of flywire screens on our old fibro house.

The dog is on my chest, standing above me and blocking out the dark sky. I look hard into his one good eye to show him I am not afraid, even now when I really should be. I think about how it should end and wish it was not in a dusty car park in some nowhere town. Not with this dog.

Suddenly there is a whirl of stick and fur and teeth and the chainsaw snarl of warring hounds, a yelping like whippets shrieking into caves. On my chest, the dog's breath escapes him in one big rush. He breaks sideways, collapsing in a pile of mange and distemper.

As he falls, the other dogs do too. They bite at each other and their own tails. Their huge yellow teeth catch the light of far off lamps. They are confused and angry, snapping at anything that moves. Finally, they break ranks and run and we are left for a moment watching a tuft of fur drift slowly to the dirt.

The egg-eyed dog is belly-up in the car park. His head is lolled back and his throat is open to the sky. His teeth are chipped and yellow, his tongue escaping his mouth. I shouldn't feel sorry for him; he wanted to kill me. I shouldn't feel anything.

In the middle of the silence is a woman. She is a foot-and-a-fart high and looks about a hundred and ten years old. She is holding a thick stick like she knows how to swing it. She tucks a stray hair behind her ear.

'Thanks,' I say.

She stares at me for a moment, her black eyes opening and closing like shutters. '*Jalan*,' she says and, turning, walks away.

I ask Niagara, 'What should we do?'

'I don't know, man. Are we supposed to follow?'

The old lady turns again and points into the dark with her stick. '*Jalan*,' she says again.

Niagara and I look at each other.

'Your mouth is bleeding,' he says.

Touching the corner of my lip, I bring a fingertip of blood to the light. 'It's nothing.'

I hammer the door of the bus and, when the driver opens up, I grab my pack and my board and we take off after the stick lady.

She turns down a street and then through a market. Everything is for sale – boyband posters, electric sanders, hair colour, peanuts, machetes, chillies, salt in woven reed containers. The old lady stops at a stall and buys some nuts. She pops a chunk in her mouth, smears her gums with white powder from a bamboo tube. Before long she is smiling a blood red smile. She offers some to us. I shake my head but Niagara nods.

'Uncle Max used to chew betel,' he says with his brain on autopilot in his uncle's dark skies.

We have seen this nut everywhere since Timor. The coral reefs are torn apart for lime; betel palms are raided for the nuts. Women are into it big-time. It turns their teeth red and makes them spit like camels. It's like smoking dope for people who favour red teeth over red eyes.

Niagara takes a bit of lime and a hunk of nut. The old woman slaps him hard on the back and Niags nearly coughs it up. The old girl is not as frail as she looks.

We continue on. Past the 'Helen Salon', with its magazine posters of Princess Di's eighties hairstyle, and three grubby restaurants. We are walking out of town.

'Niagara?' I say.

He is looking at his feet, swaying as he walks.

'Niags!'

He looks up. 'Uhuh.'

'You okay?'

'Just a bit dizzy.' He spits out the betel with a gallon of red saliva.

'You'll be fine, man. It hasn't done her any harm.' I nod to Granny marching up ahead. He tries to focus on her, then at me. We start following her again.

'Hey, Niags?'

'Yo!'

'Do you know where we are going?'

'Uh, nope.'

'Or why we are following this old granny into a very dark place?'

'Nope.'

'Me neither.'

But we keep on going because we don't know the way back to the bus. Granny and her wonderstick seem like the safest option right now.

We end up slipping like splinters into the jungle. Granny knows where she is going and every now and then she stops and waits for us to catch up. My backpack and board slap trees as we walk. There isn't much light getting in here, a bit of moon and the odd skerrick of star. Soon we are walking in a chain – me holding Granny's stick and Niagara clutching at the tail of my shirt. I wonder how I get myself into these things. It's like closing a cable tie a notch at a time – you can't undo it, and it always ends up tighter than you planned.

We come to a set of steps and Granny pulls us slowly up on the end of her stick. She opens a too-creaky door and fumbles with a box of matches. For a while that is the only sound, the rattle and slow scrape of matches. I turn my head, trying to hear something, desperate for clues. The tang of sulphur burrows through the dark and then there is a roar as a match explodes in flame. Edging it into a lamp, Granny lights the wick.

We are in a small room. There is a carved mask on the wall, a drum with a thin waist and leather skin. David Beckham's poster grin curls beside a life size pic of the Virgin Mary. A sea-blue headscarf tumbles into the borders, her red heart burns through clothing.

Granny shows us a small couch, pats the cushions for us to sit down. She smiles at Niagara and me as we ease in beside each other. We smile back. Silence creeps around the walls. I study my feet. A dog barks in the distance, the noise shuttling through trees. Belacan pricks up his ears. Finally, Granny leaves us alone, closing the door behind her.

'Man, this is freaky,' says Niagara.

'On the bizarre side,' I admit.

'This is your fault you know, Gurg. We shoulda stayed on the bus. Uncle Max wouldn't have got into this situation.'

'It's not a *situation*, Niagara.'

'Well, what the hell is it then?'

'It's just a sort of adventure-thing. We'll be fine. This is better than the bus. It was going nowhere in a hurry.'

'And now we are stuck here while Granny turns into a wolf and eats us.'

I laugh at Niagara's joke. It makes him feel good and it covers the fact that I am more than a little worried about this *situation*. What is this old chook's deal?

She returns with a bowl of boiled bananas and cups of sweet black tea. She puts them on the table in front of us. We stare at them. She smiles.

'*Makan. Minum,*' she says.

I think this means 'eat and drink' or 'drink and eat' or 'I am about to boil you alive and eat your hearts'.

She pushes the bowl of bananas nearer to us and Niagara takes one. Uncle Max must have feasted on them; the guy is following him blindly.

'Not bad, Granny,' he says through a mouthful. 'Tastes kinda like potato.' He grabs his cup of tea and slurps. 'Mmm, mm.'

Granny smiles. That's it for conversation.

We are stalemated like this for hours and I am pretty sleepy when there is a scuffle on the verandah. The doorknob rattles and the door creaks open like the gate to hell.

There is a figure silhouetted by the rising moon. It steps through the doorway and into the light. It becomes a rastafarian, with grungy dreadlocks spilling from his knitted cap.

He cranks up Bob Marley's *Legend* and lights a joint. I take a token puff but this whole thing is way too strange for me to relax and get ripped with this dude. Niagara has given himself up to the moment. He is living it like Uncle Max, getting stoned and hanging out with the locals.

The guy is Granny's grandson Robert.

'Jus call me Bob, mun,' he says.

He's just finished Tourism High School in Bajawa and wants to go to Jamaica or Jakarta and start a reggae band. He pulls out a guitar and plays along, badly, to *No Woman, No Cry*. He tries to sing but the joint gets in the way and he almost torches his dreadlocks.

Niagara is being swallowed by the couch. 'Granny is the cat's pyjamas, dude.'

'Yah, mun,' says Bob, fully in character.

'She's tops,' I say. 'Saved us from a pack of dogs.'

'She's allus doin dat, mun,' says Bob, shaking his dreads.

'What's her name?' I ask over the music.

Bob turns to me, his pupils big as winter moons. 'She be a witch, you know,' he whispers.

That wasn't what I asked but who cares.

'No shit!' I say.

'No chit, mun. A witch. Dat's why she brung you here – to do some witchin stuff on you.'

This guy has obviously smoked half his brain out of existence. 'And her name is . . .?' I try again.

'Imaculata,' says Bob.

'What a mouthful, dude.' Niagara's face cracks into a watermelon smile.

Bob leans forward so his dreads form a bead curtain in front of his eyes. He hisses, 'She knows future tings. Bet she knowed you was comin.'

'Uhuh,' says Niagara. 'Right on. Right on.' He nods.

'Nenek!' calls Bob and Granny appears from the back room. She comes out of the shadow with a scarf in her hair and her skin glowing gold with the light of the lamps. She looks directly at me.

Niagara looms into her vision and says, 'Ole Niagara wants to know if he'll find Uncle Max.'

But Granny gently pushes him aside. He crumples to the floor and chuckles softly. She stares at me. I have a feeling she isn't going to need tea-leaves or tarot cards or chicken's innards to tell my future.

She shuts her eyes for a moment. Her lids are as smooth as pistachio shells. They snap open and she starts to talk, rattling like a train heading for a derailment. She keeps going faster and faster. A moth flies around the lamp, dragging big shadows around the walls.

Niagara drags himself from the floor. 'Ask her about Uncle Max,' he says to Bob, but Bob ignores him and keeps listening to Granny.

She is looking at me, only at me. I feel like I am spinning down into her eyes, like they are whirlpools drawing everything in. The lamp goes out. The moth has entered its flame. I can smell it burning. Niagara says, 'Holy shit!' Belacan whimpers. But Granny keeps on going. I am sure I can see her eyes but it is pitch black in here. Rain starts to hit the roof outside. Granny's voice rises and falls like groundswell. She is the centre of the storm. A dot of calm in the middle of chaos. Slowly, I can make out her outline. She is twisted like an old tree, fingers branching to the ceiling. Her words are falling hard as hail, pounding my ears so I have to push my fingers in them to make it bearable. She is laughing and shouting and crying out. She is crouched like a stone. She is on the tips of her toes. Her arms are wide, gathering the static from the room, sweeping cobwebs from the charcoal corners.

Then she stops and there is only the rain. It slaps the corrugated iron like bullets. Bob lights the lamp again. Granny smiles at me like she doesn't know what's going on. Her scarf is on her knees and her hair is messed-up. She closes her eyes and takes three deep breaths of burnt moth and warm damp leaves from outside. Then she stands and walks, bent-backed, from the room. We call goodnight after her, but the rain is too loud and she doesn't reply.

'What did she say?' I ask Bob.

'Did she tell you about Uncle Max?' asks Niagara from where he had crawled to safety behind the couch.

'Uncle Max, nothing,' says Bob. 'Only about you, Goog.'

'Well, what did she say.'

'She said you will fall into de sea. Dat water is your big enemy *and* your true friend. She said dat you will find who you are not looking for. She said stop trying so hard.'

'Is that all?'

Bob nods. 'Yah, mun.'

'She took all that time and all those words to say that?'

'Yah.'

I don't believe him and I don't believe the horseshit about finding someone I am *not* looking for. As for the falling into the sea thing, well it doesn't take a witch to work that out. My board is right there in the corner. I fall into the sea every other day. Bob and Granny are full of crap. Especially the bit about not trying too hard. That is the biggest nugget of all.

'We have to go,' I say to Bob.

'Do we?' says Niagara.

'We have a bus to catch.'

'Not till tomorrow.'

'We could miss it if we stay here all night spliffing-up and listening to reggae.'

'Sleep here,' says Bob and pulls a couple of thin cotton mattresses from under the couch.

I am too tired to argue. It's raining outside and not a good time of the night to find another place to sleep. I place my postcards from Castro under my pillow and draw my towel over me.

*****

Castro is a shadow and I am trying to grasp him. He is slipping through my fingers like water. I try to capture him in an old Bintang bottle but it leaks and soaks my backpack. I reach in and pull out my Lonely Planet. There on page 31 under 'History' is a picture of Castro. I try to make out the caption but it is written in Indonesian. Then I hold it up to a mirror and discover I can read it.

> *Mark Fidle, known as Castro to his many friends, was taken by a shark while surfing in Australia. Greg 'Goog' Leary continues to search for him.*

I look at the picture again. I took it after a dawnie at *Cathedral Rock*. Aldo is in the background, solid and stupid as a post. I scan Castro's face for a clue. He shimmers and disappears. I follow him to page 167 'Java', through 'Bali' (pages 376 to 504), up again to 'Sumatra', down through 'Lombok'. He twists and turns through 'Sumbawa' and 'Flores' and drops like a pebble into the Timor Sea. I dive under but it is so dark and he is made of shadow. There are sharks here. I know the knives of their teeth and the rasp of their skin. I feel their snouts nudging my ribs, trying to get a piece of me. There is something green, big like a blanket. It wraps around me and I close my eyes.

*****

The rooster dawn whips me awake. My body is mangled from sleeping on this cotton mattress. I would have been better off in the bus. Niagara is snoring. Belacan is licking his toes, unaware of the danger from poisoning. I reach over and flick Niagara on the neck. He wakes up.

'Wha? Wha?' he says.

'Time to get up, Niags. We gotta bus to catch.'

'What time is it?'

I show him the suntan mark where my watch used to be.

'That late, huh.'

We get our gear together and are about to sneak out when Granny comes out of the kitchen with a plastic bag of bananas and biscuits. She smiles as she hands it to Niagara and pats me on the back of the hand. I try to give her some rupes for the bed and food but she shakes her head.

We can see town from Granny's verandah and we break through the forest towards it. It is a spanker of a day. The rain that fell last night has washed all the dust from the trees. I shake the stiffness from my legs and arms as I walk. I feel my spine stretching.

We return to where we abandoned the bus last night but all that remains is a big island of gear oil and clumps of dog hair.

'Now what?' says Niagara.

We flag down a ute outside of Bajawa. We travel in the tray with six goats and a twenty-litre tub of petrol. I am glad Niagara doesn't smoke. It's ten hours to Labuhanbajo.

5 Dragons and jellyfish clouds

Pulau Komodo, Flores

We are in the middle of the strait separating the islands of Flores and Sumbawa. I am edging closer to Lakey Beach. If Castro has come this way he will have stopped there. The surf is too good, the break far too legendary for him to miss catching a wave on his passage through. Plus, each time the postcards from Castro arrive I compare them with every photo shoot in every surf mag I can lay my hands on. *Lakey Peak* is a good match with one that arrived in January.

Niagara is following his dead uncle along the same road. Things are working out for us.

We made Labuhanbajo, the port of the sea-gypsies, by nightfall, two days, one bus, one banana truck and one ute after leaving Larantuka – at the far end of Flores. We slept for a day and felt like we were coming down from a bad trip.

This morning, we jumped on the Karaoke Ferry bound for Komodo. Now I am wedged between two pop-eyed guys playing cards on my lap while Leo Sayer sings *When You Need Me* above the bouncing white dot on the TV screen. These men have Lipovita energy drink bottles hanging from their ears by cotton string. They are focussed on my lap where hearts, diamonds, clubs and spades are falling.

My board is being used as a dining table by a family of Javanese Muslims. The cover is sticky with rice, with chicken and vegetables dripping yellow oil.

Niagara is at the side of the boat staring at the islands as if they contain some clue to Uncle Max. I don't know what he is looking for, or why he is so caught up with finding it, but I am sure he thinks the same of me. I guess no one leaves home if they have all the answers. If they are happy, they stay put.

The boat grunts and shudders. It stops and my stomach keeps moving on, hypnotised by three hours of sea motion. The cards in my lap fall onto the floor, followed by the Lipovita bottles.

'We're here!' shouts Niagara. He grabs his sack in one hand, Belacan in the other, and leaps over the side of the boat.

I run to the edge, hoping to see him floundering in the water but instead he is climbing down from the roof of a smaller boat – the 'passenger link' to Komodo Island. I shoulder my pack and grab my table-board from the feasting Javanese. They smile and wave their yellow palms at me as I leave.

This boat is much smaller and full of sweating Kiwis trying to clamber up to the ferry for the trip on to Sumbawa.

'Thus us bloody ruduculous!' they are shouting.

'Guv us a hand, wull yus.'

Eventually they get all their Macpac and Fairydown gear onto the ferry and, flipping their fingers at our boatman, they go inside for a beer and some Leo Sayer classics.

And then we are off too. Through the swirling waters of the strait and towards Komodo – home of the big-arse lizard.

Heronimus is our guide. 'You can call me Hero,' he says and shoots a super-cool look at the two South African girls. He has a big stick, a machete and a moustache that has done time as a shoe brush.

'Ora is very fierce. Very, very. I protect you,' says Hero as we stomp the dusty path away from our cabins and into the heart of Komodo. 'This tree,' says Hero, pulling down a branch. 'That mountain,' he says pointing at a hill. 'We go this way.'

And we struggle to keep up with him.

'He's fast, this bugger,' says one of the South Africans. She has dark hair and a pair of reflective sunnies perched on her head.

'I don't think he wants to meet a lizard,' I whisper to her.

Hero scowls at us and says, 'Quiet. You scare Ora.'

'They don't sound very dangerous if whispering spooks them,' says the girl with the sunnies. She pulls them down over her pale green eyes to shield herself from the Hero power-stare.

We stop under a clump of wattles. There is a fat dragon in a mottled patch of sunlight. He doesn't look dangerous. He looks bored. Belacan eases his snout out of Niagara's sack. He sniffs the dragon-filled air, then drops back inside to sleep.

Hero pokes the dragon with his stick. 'Ora,' he says. 'Komodo Dragon. Poisonous sting.'

'Actually,' says the other girl, the one without the glasses, 'the bite isn't venomous. It's their saliva. It's full of bacteria that turns the wound septic.'

Hero ignores her. She isn't as good looking as the girl with the sunnies and she knows too much. 'These claw,' he picks up a lazy foot with his stick. 'Can rip a man in twice, or woman. One bite can chop an arm. Very dangerful, this one.' He pokes him again and the dragon turns his head side on so he can fully appreciate Hero and his heroics.

Niagara opens Uncle Max's diary and reads,

ENTER THE DRAGON

he so laconic
fat, full of sun
blink one eye
claws the size of fingers

head an old shoebox
from where he brings
the split string
of his pink tongue

this man with stick
so clever
poke, poke
so clever
ha, ha
big joke

big lizard quick

I like this one, too, because it means something. I like the fact that the lizard can get one over on the man with the stick. Plus it pisses off Hero.

'No good,' he says. 'Dragon shamed, angry. He bite you, Mr Merika.'

'I'm not American,' says Niagara and points to his three-day-old I'M AN AUSSIE, YES I AM! T-shirt.

'Hmh!' snorts Hero and gives the sleepy dragon a whack on the tail with his stick. The dragon is shocked into action. Niagara is in front of him.

We are at the first aid station at Loh Liang. The teeth marks are dark purple and the skin is bruised around them. It's nasty but the doctor has cleaned it out and given Niagara some antibiotics. She thinks he'll be okay. Hero left quickly on a tourist boat for Sumbawa. He will be in the shit if he ever comes back.

The girls are concerned and Niagara is loving the attention. The one with the sunnies is Beck. Urs is a nurse from Jo'burg.

'I know, it sounds like a kids book,' she says.

Niagara is running a fake fever and Urs is bringing him cold 7 UP and face washers. I walk down to the pier with Beck.

All these conversations start the same, 'Where you from? Where you going? How long have you been travelling?' I should have it tattooed on my forehead. But I like this girl; she is cool and gutsy. I like the way she walks with her palms facing backwards and her eyes scanning the sky as if something good is going to come from there at any moment. She is not bad looking either. And I like her accent, the way she clips her words so they have sharp, crisp edges.

'Do you miss home?' she asks as we get to the water.

I pick up a stone and skim it over the bay. It sinks into the last wide circle and I say, 'Not much. Torquay is a small place and we outgrew it.' I really mean Castro outgrew it, but I am too afraid to speak his name. Not here. Not now.

'I'm going to travel forever,' says Beck as she lies on her stomach to reach the high tide. The hollow in her back has the finest blonde hairs I have ever seen.

I snap myself back. 'You gotta touch base sometime,' I say, not really thinking about what I have said.

'Why?' she asks.

'I dunno.' And I don't but I feel I have to defend what I have just said. 'You belong there. Plus, family is important. And friends.'

'They can come and see me if they want to,' she says and, slipping forward, falls neatly into the clear water. I watch as she swims down and then rises in a smooth arc for the surface, bursting through in a shower of mercury coins.

Niagara's wound gets weepy and he becomes a pain in the arse. Even more of a pain in the arse than usual. Urs the nurse works with old people – grumpy old people – and she says that Niagara is worse than all of them wired together. We are stuck on Komodo until Niagara gets well. I should be keen to keep moving, to find Castro, but it is comfortable to just hang out here with Beck. We walk down to the pier and skim stones. We swim. She never asks me what I want out of life, not once.

We walk in the forest – me armed with a big stick, Beck with her smile.

She asks, 'How come they call you Goog?'

I shrug.

'Does it mean anything?' She raises her sunnies so I can see her eyes.

'Goog means "egg". It's an old Aussie word for egg. Aussies

are mad for nicknames, everyone's got to have one, it's a rule. Sometimes they mean something, sometimes not.'

'Egg, huh?'

I nod.

She pokes me in the chest. 'Hard shell, but soft inside.'

I don't know where she is going with this. 'My name's Greg. I think I just copped the nickname cause it sounds a bit like Greg. Greg, egg, googy-egg, Goog!'

She lowers her glasses, twists on her toes and walks away.

There is no surf in Komodo but I paddle my board out into the bay and past the point, bearded with stunted palms. Beck swims behind me, hanging onto the legrope when she gets tired. She is wearing a bottle-green bikini and her body is brown as oiled wood. I make excuses to look at her.

We arrive at a reef where the water is so clear we can see the stupid, colourful fish turning around the coral heads, bumping into each other, snapping at shadows. All this glassy blue water is beautiful but useless. Sumba shields Komodo from swell. I picture the point with six-footers wrapping round into our bay. I would stay here forever.

Beck can't see my point of view. She reckons I should live for the moment and appreciate what we have. She has never been to *J-Bay*, or *Cape St Francis* on the cold water coast. These South African breaks are legendary to surfers, but to Beck they mean nothing. She likes movies and she paints and she reads the future in the sky.

She points to a puffy white cloud. 'The Jellyfish,' she says. 'Floats on top of the water without looking below.'

This isn't really true, I have seen jellyfish floating under the water too, but I don't interrupt.

She continues, hamming it up like a fortune-teller, putting on a weird Russian accent. 'You veel travelll a long, long times but you veel only scratch ze surface unless you dive beneaths ze votter.'

'What does that mean?' I ask. She is as bad as Granny Imaculata in Bajawa.

She smiles. We are resting on my board, our bodies dangling above the reef. Pushing off, she twists backwards into the water and swims down.

I take a deep breath and swim after her. Below the surface everything is blurred. The fish are blobs of colour, the coral just bulky shadows. I see a flash of bottle-green and chase it. It disappears behind a coral head and I follow. I go deeper and deeper. My eyes sting. The oxygen goes stale in my lungs and my chest starts to burn. I reach the head, spiral around it looking for her. She isn't there. I paddle up to the surface, exploding into the air and sucking it in. There is no sign of Beck, not a ripple or a bubble.

There is no way she could hold her breath for this long. What if she is tangled in the reef? A breeze springs up and ruffles the sea making it hard to see below. I take another dive but there are only fish and coral heads. Shit! Why did she do this? I picture her body limp and bloated with water. I dive again. My arms and legs ache from fear and lack of air, my body is being poisoned. I go for the surface.

She is there. Lying on her back, on my board, reading the clouds as if nothing has changed.

'Beck?'

'Hey, Goog.'

'Where did you get to?' I try to be cool but there is something that feels like a fishhook in my throat.

She looks at me, shades her eyes with her hand. 'I just had a bit of a swim around.'

'You scared the shit out of me, Beck!' There is no calmer way of saying it.

'I'm okay, Goog. I can take care of myself. You got to learn to relax, boy.'

I kiss her when it is dark. We are up in the forest, behind the lodge, with cool Bintangs. She tastes of hops and salt. She leans into me and I feel the softness of her skin, her tight stomach and her breasts.

I clear away the rocks and we lie in the leaf litter and look at the stars winking at us from behind the branches.

'There are Ora,' says Beck, trying to scare me, trying to sound like Hero.

'Very dangerful,' I say and kiss her again. I want her to come to my cabin but I know Niagara is there, lying on the bed, his wound weeping like a creek onto the sheets.

I try to unbutton Beck's dress. But she says, 'Not here.

Down by the sea.' She takes my hand and we sneak past the cabins and down to the pier. The sky clouds over and she shivers. I cover her with my body. She is like dropping into water.

Beck's SLR camera is guts-open on the table. There are tiny springs, their wire as fine as horsehair, and small screws sitting in upturned bottle tops. Every one of them is in order. I have drawn a quick sketch on a napkin in case I forget where they belong.

'How did you get so good at this?' asks Beck.

I pick up my beer and take a quick sip, not taking my eyes from her Nikon for too long. 'My dad was into mechanics. He was forever pulling our car apart. He taught me a few tricks. And I used to be into photography. Guess it's just a short hop from cars to cameras.'

'How come you don't have a camera now?'

Slowly, I ease the shutter leaves over with a matchstick. They are jamming slightly and I need to be careful. I can feel Beck's breath on my neck. The leaves move.

'There,' I say and, after withdrawing the match carefully, press the shutter release. The Nikon gives a solid click and the shutter moves open and shut. I twist the aperture ring round and check the iris is opening and closing properly.

'You didn't answer my question,' says Beck.

'I guess the camera wasn't as important as this trip. I had to decide. I needed a ticket, so I sold my camera.'

'Did that camera mean a lot to you?'

'I won it in a photo comp. It was a good unit.' I turn Beck's Nikon over. It is a good camera too. 'Some people thought I could go places with my photography.'

'What people?'

I begin to reassemble, looping the tiny springs in with Niagara's tweezers, screwing the plates into place. 'Just people.'

'An ex-girlfriend?'

I am turning fully beetroot but I don't understand why. It's not as if Beck would mind if I had a girlfriend. I bend closer to the camera to hide my face. 'Yeah, a *very* ex-girlfriend. Plus, my mum and my old teachers thought I should do photography at uni.'

I twist the last screw home and load a film. Beck smiles as I hand her the camera.

'You should keep it,' she says, putting her other hand over the top of mine.

'No, it's yours. I can't take it.'

'I can't even use it properly. Everything comes out dark.'

'You probably haven't set your film speed,' I say.

'I'd rather paint,' says Beck, but she takes the Nikon and slides it into her daypack.

*****

He has long fingers. They are tapping on glass. His face is as big as the moon and twice as yellow, cheese rind gone wrong.

He has pole-vaulter's legs, tall-timber swaying up to his orange vest.

'I am the coyote, boy . . . I am the coyote . . .' he chants over and over. It becomes thunder, rolling hard over a churning sea and I am a stone, slipping sideways, hidden by weed and rock and shadow stripes but I am a human heart filled with ocean, gripped in his narrow fingers, wrapped around like octopus tentacles, and he is a giant squid, tackling my boat, dragging it under and I am screaming, covered in blood and scales and he is jerking me, wires across my body, tied into my palms and feet, and my joints are screwed, my eyes are holes of burning light, I am thin as a slip of paper, scared if I turn sideways I will be lost so I yell and yell and yell until my throat burns . . .

*****

'Goog!' Beck is bent over me, her hair haloed by the moon. 'It's just a dream, Goog. Just a dream.'

My breath is jackhammering my chest and I am shaking, but her hands are as soft as a spring tide. The boards of the pier are smooth beneath me.

'You want to talk about it?' she asks.

I shake my head. I don't want to talk about Jasper; that is what powers him, makes him real. It is better that he stays in my nightmares, where he belongs. These dreams have stalked me for over a year – since the day he crashed into our lives. One day I will find him and exorcise his demon, plunge a stake into his evil heart.

'Let's go swimming,' says Beck.

'But it's night.'

'The best time,' says Beck and, before I can stop her, she dives from the pier.

'Come back,' I call, but I can hear her stroking for the other side of the inlet. I jump into the water, feet first, feeling the salty rush in my nose. I rise and follow her wake.

We kiss. She is slippery as eelgrass. Her hair gets in my mouth. She pulls me down and the water is warm and there is only her. The world above is nothing.

'No way, Gurg.' Niagara is sitting in the restaurant with Belacan on his knee feeding him two-minute noodles with a spoon. 'Nopenopenope!'

'Come on, mate, be reasonable.'

'Reasonable don't even come into it. She ain't coming and that's that. Three's a crowd, Gurg, three is a crowd.'

'But that's what I'm trying to tell you, Urs is coming as well, Urs the nurse.' I slap Niagara on the arm, the bad arm, the leaky-weepy arm. Bad move.

'Sheeeet, Gurg! Waddarya trying todoodoomee.' His teeth are clenched and he's dropped a spoonful of noodles on Belacan.

'Sorry, man. Just trying to be friendly.'

'Look, we already got enough along on this expedition. Me, you, Belacan, Uncle Max, Castro. What are we trying to do here? Build an army?'

'Beck is coming along whether you are or not.'

'Well that's it, Gurg. This is where we part company.'

Suits me fine. Loudmouth bastard.

I ignore him and he ignores me. Urs the nurse wanders up from her cabin. 'What's news?' she asks.

'Ask Gurg,' snarls Niagara.

'I told him that you and Beck were coming with us.'

Urs puts her hands on her hips. 'Did you now.'

'Well, Beck said you'd want to come along.'

'And who died and made her queen?'

'I just thought you'd—'

'I'll see about this.' Urs turns and stomps to their cabin, mushroom clouds opening in the dust of her footprints.

This is not going well. I grab my board and head down to the water. I get to the pier and strap on my leggie. There is no way I need a leash but it feels good to go through the motions, to pretend that I might be paddling out to some break. Almost a week and a half in Indonesia and not a single wave. Craziness. I leap out from the pier. It is high tide and there's not much of a drop. The water feels cool and clean. I sip a little just to taste the salt.

I paddle around the point and past the reef where Beck did her disappearing act. A green turtle swims beneath me and I keep pace with it for a while until it gives a burst with its flippers and rockets off. Then I follow the sleek shape of a fish, shadowing it like a shark. When I lose it, I tail another, and then another until there is an unbroken chain of follow-my-leader zigzagging nearly all the way to Loh Liang. And then I look up and don't recognise anything.

I figure if I am paddling around an island and I keep going in one direction I will eventually arrive where I started – back at Loh Liang. There is a long way and a short way in this game. The short way will take me back the way I came. The long way will lead right around the island. I try to remember how big Pulau Komodo is. With Pulau Rinca – the other dragon island – it took up a good half page in the Lonely Planet. I have no idea of the scale. These are the things I do know: it is hot; I have no water; and no one knows where I am. Bad things always come in threes.

I keep paddling, scanning the shore for clues where there is nothing but blank rock faces and straggle-haired trees and the white-hot sun arcing off everything. Maybe I could go overland, maybe I should, but there are too many paths to choose from, too many ways to go wrong and there are the dangerful Ora, waiting with their big teeth slick with poisonous spit, and these islands are very dry, not much more than hot rocks with a few burnt shrubs struggling along on top – where do those plants get enough water to keep them alive? – and the sun is a fire on my back and I can feel the layers of skin being stripped as I paddle and look and hope and turn to shore then stay away from the rocks where dragons are waiting for me. Rolling off my board, I drop into the water and it touches me like ice and I imagine a hiss as my skin drops from boiling to freezing. I shiver and float on my back and search the clouds for clues as the water sucks at my ears. Someone calls my name and I jerk upright in the water, but there are no boats, and nothing on shore. It was Beck, I am sure, but she is nowhere in sight.

Back on my board, it takes minutes for the water to dry leaving a crackly salt crust over my shoulders and on my eyebrows and I rub it off and put some on my tongue where it sits and stings. I am way thirsty and can't keep my mind from the cold drinks at Loh Liang – 7 UP, Coke, Bir Bintang – all on ice, served in a glass at a table with a fan ruffling my hair and I can taste the bottled water, cool and oh-so safe, all those times I ignored it in favour of beer or soft drink and I wish myself home, drinking straight from the garden hose, litres of the stuff pouring off my chin and down my chest.

I lie still letting the waves tut-tut against the bottom of my board, feeling the energy leaking out of me, the soles of my feet burning, the soft skin behind my knees peeling like heated paint.

If I died of thirst out here who would know? I wouldn't even leave a mark on the surface of the ocean if I slipped under quietly like a stone returning to the seabed, a cold, cold stone. Would dead-arse Castro look for *me*? Would Mum call in the Navy Seals? Would it lure Dad from wherever the hell he is hiding? Would Beck cry? She has only known me for three days. Would she keep going as if nothing had happened?

I shake it all off and keep paddling.

The sun begins to drop behind the island and I hug the coast where there are deep patches of shade that cool my body. The colour leaches from the sea, the rocks and the trees. My dad once told me he had watched a man die. It was in Vietnam and he had caught a tracer bullet in the stomach. He said it was the man's lips that surprised him most, that they looked like the end of the day when the sun steals the colour. That story has always stayed with me – it was the only thing he told me about Vietnam – and it returns now as I look at the sloping grey-blue rocks on the shore. Dad smelled of rolling tobacco and peppermints. His hands were callused, the size of wicket-keeper's gloves. He would hold me in the ocean and I was safer then than I have ever been since.

Darkness drums down on the ocean, flattening the dying light over Pulau Komodo and forcing stars into the sky. I don't know if I am going in circles. Birds crash through the trees on shore, squawking and fighting for positions on branches. Then I see a faint yellow glow from beyond the next point and, as I round it, I see lights and hear the thrum of a generator.

The lights are spread along the dark line of the shore. They push out to the ocean and reflect on the black plate of the sea. I could be swimming through stars as I paddle up to the beach.

I don't know how long I have been in the water. The bananas I swapped for my watch are long gone, crapped to nothing. I rub my fingers together and feel the roughness of wrinkled ridges on them. My body is drenched with salt. My joints ache. Beck, Niagara and Urs are probably out looking for me. They will have hired a boat and be scanning the sea with torches, expecting to see me floating face-down.

I walk up the beach with my board. The smell of sewage and kerosene hits me as I crunch towards the village. I pass fishermen with lamps and clouds of soft net under their arms. They peer into my face, smile uncomfortably, rattle quiet words to each other.

'Loh Liang?' I say to them, but they just nod.

The village is full of nasty dogs with open wounds and shit-crusted arses. I pick up a stick with my free hand. The main street is dirt, laced with broken glass and bottle tops. My bare feet don't seem like enough. Dark doorways hold eyes that keep me moving. I pass a tin-shack mosque with fairy lights strung to the crescent moon on its dome. There is a group of men squatted in the doorway.

'Loh Liang?' I ask them. They point to where I came from.

I am about to move on when a voice calls me. 'Sir. Sir.'

A boy of about ten or eleven with a Marlboro T-shirt pushes past the men in the doorway of the mosque. 'Loh Liang?' he asks.

'Yes. Loh Liang. I . . . need . . . to . . . go . . . there.' I figure if I speak slowly enough he'll understand.

He shakes his head and laughs. 'Loh Liang?' he says again.

'Yes. Loh . . . Liang.' He may just be messing with my head here. Maybe he has no idea where it is. Maybe I have paddled to another island.

'Yar. Yar. Loh Liang. Loh Liang.' He starts to walk down the street. Do I follow? I look at the squatted mosque-men. They flap their hands at me. '*Jalan! Jalan!*' they say. '*Cepat!*'

So I follow Mosque-boy. He moves quickly down the street with his Jellybean sandals. They are fluorescent pink. He knows everyone in the village. He struts, calls out to his mates, whacks an unlucky dog with a stick. I catch up with him, slaloming between patches of splintered bottle.

He looks me up and down. 'Ischmoke?' he asks.

'What?'

'Ischmoke!' He mimes very speedy chain-smoking.

'You are way too young, mate,' I say, shaking my head.

'Ischmoke!' he screams. Old men and mothers come to the windows of their shacks. They stare at me like I have done something bad to Mosque-boy and if I don't watch out they will get their kitchen knives and their bodybuilder sons.

Mosque-boy stops at a shop; a wooden shack with its shutters hung with shampoo sachets and blurry magazines. He points to an open packet of Gudang Garam cigarettes. 'Ischmoke.'

The woman behind the counter taps a bent fag from the packet. I show her my empty palms, pat the pocket of my boardies. No money. She squeezes the cigarette back into place. Mosque-boy shakes his head and wanders back towards the mosque. I run after him.

'Wait, kid. Wait!' I am like a ballerina on this shattered glass street. My heels don't touch the ground.

He ignores me and keeps on walking. Little bastard! I grab him by the shoulder and spin him around. He pulls his fists in front of his face and bounces on his feet like a boxer.

'Mate,' I say, dodging his punches. 'You gotta get me to Loh Liang. I can't go back in the water, it's too dark. My friends will be worried about me. They'll be out looking.'

'Ischmoke,' he says, dropping his fists.

'Yes. Yes. *Ischmoke* at Loh Liang,' I lie. None of us smoke.

'Ischmoke Loh Liang?'

'Uhuh! Loh Liang. Plenty *ischmoke*, cartons of the bloody things. Truckloads!' My head is nodding itself off my shoulders.

He nods and starts off down the street again, away from the mosque and hopefully towards Loh Liang.

The track is pitch black and full of night noises.

I ask Mosque-boy, 'Ora?'

'Ora *tidur*,' he says and makes a snoring noise.

Mosque-boy has no torch and how he sees this track is a miracle. Stars wink at us through the forest canopy but I can't even see my bare feet. It is hard going with my board and I want to dump it and come back for it in the morning. The only snag is that I would never find my way back here and even if I did Mosque-boy would have pawned it for a carton of Gudangs.

My feet start to hurt and the rocks turn into razors. My board snags on vines and I keep whacking my head on low branches. This track seems to go on forever. And then we burst out of the jungle and I can hear music and see puddles of light.

'Loh Liang,' says Mosque-boy. 'Ischmoke?'

I go to my room and give him ten thousand rupiah. He can choof himself silly with that. I watch him disappear into the forest then seek out the others. They might have called off the search for the night. From the restaurant, the Backstreet Boys are pounding in stereo. Accompanied by Niagara's high-pitched laugh. From outside I can see him, Urs and Beck sitting at a table. They are surrounded by a platoon of empty Bintangs.

I walk casually up the steps and into the restaurant. I am burned raw from the sun and covered in salt crust and dirt.

'Gurg!' Niagara shouts. 'Siddown. Pull up a beer, my man.'

The waiter comes over and waits.

'Water, thanks,' I croak. 'Bottled water.'

Urs and Beck laugh. Beck's sunglasses are crooked on her head, Urs is swaying to the Backstreet Boys.

'Where have you been?' Beck asks, pulling her head in and out of focus.

'I went for a swim.'

Niagara slaps me on my sunburnt back. 'Gurg! We had a bit of a pow-wow while you were gone. Decided to travel together.'

Three beery smiles. Six cloudy eyes, eyebrows high.

'That's great, guys. Really good.' The waiter brings my water and I toast the latest recruits to our *army*.

6 Wild water dance

Sape–Dompu, Sumbawa

We are on our way to Dompu. There is nothing there. It is a bus terminal town – a couple of banks, some roundabouts, a few beat-up trucks and stuff-all else. The Lonely Planet is no big raps for the place. What we are aiming for is at Lakey Beach, a peak that grinds hard over shallow coral. This break would be a candle to Castro's moth-like ghost.

No one else wanted to stop in Sumbawa. They were all for pissing through on the night bus to Lombok. Niagara couldn't find Sumbawa anywhere in Uncle Max's journal. Urs wanted to get to some pottery town in Lombok. My search is being swamped by a sea of everyone else's wants and there is no way that's fair. Besides, my board hasn't even been near a wave since I got here and it is high time I got some Indo tube action.

Beck has written a 'Letter of Complaint' to the company who owns this bus. She reads it out.

'Letter of Complaint. Dear Director of the Jawa Baru Bus Company, I am writing in complaint of a bus trip I recently took from Sape to Gute Terminal, Dompu on the island of Sumbawa. Not only was there inadequate seating for the many people but the bus lacked even the most basic comforts, such as: padded seats, air-conditioning or complimentary meals.'

The hard, frayed seats have their backs tattooed with names – Beng Beng, Westlife, Dompu Gang.

Beck continues, 'I was also shocked to discover many passengers (and even the driver!) smoking kretek cigarettes. The driving was so erratic and the condition of the road so bad that many people vomited into plastic bags, which (to your credit) you provided. I would like to advise you, if you do not lift your standards on this service I shall be forced to seek other travel arrangements in the future. Yours Sincerely, Beck.'

Niagara gives her the thumbs-up. His dragon bite is covered with an old bandage that Urs keeps asking to change. I think he likes the way it looks – dirty and dangerous.

Salt farmers run this end of the island. Their fields are piled with pyramids of grey salt. Their backs are bent to the sun as they scrape at the dirt. Every small town and village is humming with snot-nosed kids and packs of scabby dogs. The air is full of dust and light and heat, the country is harsh and dry

– a mess of twisted hills and torn trees. I wish I was somewhere else; anywhere but here in bus limbo, passing through hell to get to wave heaven.

Leo Sayer is singing *When I Need You* on a stretched tape. Niagara hangs over our seat back and reads us a poem from Uncle Max's journal.

HOME

some days i dream of home
then forget where that is
i am alone
with the masks
of a thousand strangers
and the danger
of losing myself

Niagara looks at me. 'Do you get that?'

I shrug – what's to get – and look to Beck for a comment but she has her nose pressed against the window. I touch her shoulder and, as she turns, I notice a tear running on a strange diagonal across her cheek.

'What's up?' I ask.

'Nothing,' she answers and returns to the window.

She whispers, so I can't be sure I hear her right, 'Travel is just a complicated plan for running away.'

It is dark and we are on the back of motorbikes. Ojek, they call them – a taxi-bike, crazy dinking system that runs from the bus station at Dompu through the village of Hu'u and ends up at Lakey Beach. That's if we ever make it. We are putting our lives in the hands of halfwits who wouldn't know a road rule if it ran up and bit them on the arse.

The exhaust pipe is burning hairs from my leg and my board is flapping like a stiff sail, trying to rip me into the blackness. The night is heavy with two-stroke fumes and fat beetles that smack us like rocks.

Beck is up ahead, her arms outstretched, the wild flow of her hair in our headlight. Urs the nurse rockets by, hooting like a howler monkey. You think she'd know better, being a nurse. Surely she has seen the mangled bodies of riders in the emergency department. Her driver pulls a mono as he passes, his light burying itself in the overhead trees.

My pack is strapped to my shoulders, resting on the mudguard. Every time the driver gives it some juice, the weight of my gear tries to pull my hand from his fat belly. I twist his rolls to slow him down. He shouts something bad at me.

He wants to go faster. I can feel the jumpiness of his throttle arm through his stomach. I pinch him hard. Niagara flies past as we enter a village. His face is a yellowed mask in the glow of lamps. Belacan's ears are blown out like windsocks. This is bullshit. It's all Niagara's fault; the bastard is too much of a tightwad to fork out the rupiah for a taxi. 'Let's take ojeks,' he said. 'It'll be fun, Gurg.'

Then we are out of the trees and into open land. The sky is sprayed with stars. I can smell the sea, feel its cool tongues on my arms. I can see a glow through a field that must be the huts at Lakey Beach.

The bikes up ahead stop. They switch off their lights. We stop. The night is dark and still. I can hear bat wings and the alarm bell of a far off cicada. In the background is the pig's grunt of surf walloping a reef. The ojek gang demand money.

'Thrittytousands,' says the leader, Niag's driver. He strikes a match and I see a scar like a whiplash across his thin neck. I wonder if he has lived through a hanging. He lights his smoke and the smell of cloves empties into the space between us.

Niagara hands him thirty thousand but he points the glowing tip of his cigarette at his three mates. 'Thritty-tousands. Thrittytousands. Thrittytousands.' One, two, three.

'Uh-uh!' says Niagara. And I think I can hear the gel falling from his shaking hair. 'Nup. Nooooooway.'

'Thrittytousands,' repeats Whiplash and, taking a crackly drag on his smoke, reaches into a bag strapped to his bike.

'Here,' says Urs, stuffing some money into his free hand. 'Take it. Sixty thousand.'

I do the maths. It's only ninety thousand total and Whiplash wants one-twenty. He pulls something out of his bag. It is dark and I strain to see what it is. He comes very close to Niagara. So close that the orange glow of his kretek reflects in Niagara's eyes. Then he slips something in Niag's shirt pocket.

We walk away quickly. The bikes start up and they gun them a couple of times before screaming up the road towards Hu'u.

Niagara pulls a card out and shines a torch on it.

'Mungkin Gusthose,' he reads. 'Budget luxuries goodfood bed showers.'

'Let's go,' says Beck.

We sign in at the Mungkin Guesthouse. Under 'Occupation' I put 'surfer'. Beck signs in as 'goddess'. Niagara is a 'pornstar' and Urs decides on 'wet-nurse'. The owner shows us a couple of bungalows. She is small and untidy and her rooms are too. Niagara says, 'We'll take this one, Gurg.' I look at Beck and she just shrugs. Does Niagara think I *want* to spend the nights with him?

The girls leave and I lie on the bed and read the graffiti on the wall.

'Never pay up-front. Never put anything in the safe. Rip-offs every two months. Better go now.' And on the door 'No spongers. **Piss off you gimp mask-wearing dog. Sponging rules**.' Further down. 'BRA BOYS SUX AS MUCH AS THERE ROOTED HOMY MATES AND ALMOST AS MUCH AS A PACK OF TEN BRAZIL NUTS.'

I go outside and wander past the dingy restaurant with its single diner and wind up on the beach. The tide is low and the waves are cracking onto the reef. Heavy water shutting down, tubes spitting air into the night. It cuts something loose inside me. I feel a rush of fear and exhilaration. The first hot spurt of adrenalin shoots through my legs. Tomorrow I'll paddle out. I have been too long away from it. This trip can be more than just a search for Castro. This is my chance to hook into some Indo juice.

I feel arms around my waist. Beck's slender fingers, circling my wrists.

'You miss it, don't you?' she asks.

'Yeah, always.'

'Why did you come here, Goog?'

'Lakey's?' I ask. 'Surf, sea, sex.'

She laughs. 'No. I want to know why you came to Indonesia.'

'It was close.'

'That's not a reason.'

'Every Australian surfer comes here. It's tradition.'

'And that's it?'

Should I tell her? Will it mean something if I do? Should I show her the stack of postcards wrapped in Dad's skull-and-crossbone bandana? I look out at the patch of noisy dark and picture the waves, their hollowness, fingers of coral reaching up through their faces.

'I had a friend.'

'A friend?'

'Yeah, a real good friend. One of those from way-back-when. I knew him forever.'

'So what happened?'

I step forward onto the beach, letting Beck's arms drop away from me.

'He left.'

'Did he come to Indonesia? Is that why you're here?'

'I don't know.'

'You don't know if he came here or you don't know if that's why you're here?'

'Either.'

I don't want to mention Castro's name. I don't want to say it out loud. It might destroy everything with us. Maybe I should just forget this whole search business and just cruise with Beck.

'Let's get some food,' I say and, taking her hand, we walk away from the beach.

Derek's Bar has jaffles and twenty-four hour surf vids. It's like heaven, but louder. We watch *Mad Wax* and *Endless Summer Two*. We eat jaffles and chips and drink cold beers. We meet Derek. He is a forty-year-old Balinese guy with dolphin tattoos and an ex-wife in Perth. His name is actually Ketut. It's his son who's called Derek. His wife got the boy when they split.

The twelve-year-old waiters call us mate; they have bleached hair and Billabong shirts. 'Wannabeermite? Naow wuckers! Fire dinkam.' They bludge smokes off customers and drink dregs from bottles. They are the wild boys of Lakey Beach.

They turn up the music and Beck dances. She is beautiful and crazy; there is sweat on her upper lip. She tries to pull me onto the floor but I'm not much of a dancer so Niags gives it a shot. He looks like a wounded seagull, all wrong angles and too much jerkiness. Beck moves like a tree, a forest of kelp, a cloud.

Urs puts her hand on my arm. 'You like her, don't you?' she says.

I try to play it cool and just nod.

'Be careful, Goog. You're a good guy.'

I don't know what she means and I am too scared to ask. She is blowing ill-winds at my house of cards. And here I am, mixing up things that my old English teacher would axe me for.

I go for Bintangs and there is a bleary-eyed blond guy sitting at the bar drinking what looks like milky piss.

'Skol!' he shouts and, raising the glass at me, necks the lot, shutting his eyes tight as it motors to his stomach. When he opens them, he looks surprised to see me still standing there. Pouring another measure, he offers it to me. 'Try it, it is good.' His accent is smooth as river pebbles but foreign. I think he's European.

Urs is waiting for her Bintang and Beck and Niagara are dancing like fools. I grab the glass and chuck it down.

It is like fire and mud and the room goes dark for a moment. It hits my stomach and tries to rise but I lock my teeth behind it.

'What the hell was that?' I ask.

'Arak. From Flores, they have the best Lontar Palms there.'

'It tastes like cockie's piss.' I feel like I have eaten a handful of cigarette butts.

'Ah, yes, like piss. But the feeling is good, yes?'

The feeling is kind of weird but I take the next glass he offers and that one is okay. The next tastes good and by the fourth me and Knut are the best of mates.

'I am from Sweden,' says Knut. 'I am the Swedish Surfing Team.' He laughs at his own joke and dribbles a little arak onto his Mambo shirt – the one with the dog humping someone's leg.

Urs comes and grabs her beer, she has hooked up with a bunch of dudes from California and they are playing a drinking game at the corner table. Beck is still dancing with the Seagull. Stuff them, I think and take a shot of arak. Knut orders up another and I pay.

The crew behind the bar crank up the music and it is hard to talk. Knut teaches me some Swedish. *Tag det lungt, flicka lilla!* (Take it easy, little girl.) I repeat it over and over again. My head is buzzing off. *Tag det lungt, flicka lilla. Tag det lungt.*

Beck is still dancing with Niagara. He's a goose. The room tilts badly as I walk towards them. The bass line fights inside my head, pushing at my temples and blurring my eyes. I grab Beck from behind and spin her around. As she turns, there is shock and confusion on her face, then she smiles and loops her arms around my neck. Niagara slinks back to the table.

The Chili Peppers come on and Niagara, Urs and the Californians join us. We are shouting out lines. The floor is shaking; lizards are falling from the walls.

I want something slower, a reason to get closer to Beck. Niagara is on the floor again and doing his spastic seagull. Urs starts to dance with Beck but I grab Beck's hand and drag her out of Derek's Bar and onto the sand.

She pulls away from me. Stars are crashing together above us, and the sea is angry. 'I want to dance, Goog,' she shouts.

I need to fill the moment, keep her here. I am desperate. 'Beck,' I slur. 'I love you.'

'You what?' she says. Her hair blows over her eyes.

'I . . . I . . .'

'I heard you, Goog.'

What a dumbshit thing to say. I wish I could suck back those words but I just stand there looking at Beck with my mouth open, catching stars. And then I turn and stumble across the beach, into the darkest part of the night where even the moon will have trouble finding me.

Morning in Indo. Every day the same: sun, heat. Be a shit-easy job forecasting weather here. I spent last night on the beach and there is plenty of sand in my ears. There is sand down my pants and in my pockets and what feels like sand in my throat. My tongue is dry and my teeth feel sticky. Water is the cure – fresh and salt, in that order.

The restaurant is closed; the fridge locked with a thick

chain and padlock. I could almost gnaw my way into it. I wander to our bungalow, lie on the bed and try not to think about water.

Water. Water. Water.

Niagara is snoring with Belacan curled into the vee of his arm. The sound of hollow waves cracks in through the window. I really need some fresh sky juice.

You can drink your own piss up to three or four times – my mum told me that. One of the Indian Prime Ministers used to do it every morning. Some kind of health thing, she reckoned. I go for a leak and give it some thought, but the hot asparagus smell puts me off.

The tap plinks some cool water into the cracked basin and I stand for a while looking at it. Mum's number one rule – *DON'T DRINK THE WATER.*

Slipping my finger under the tap, I catch one drop and hold it up to the light. It glints. I am so thirsty I can feel my throat closing over. The drop looks friendly and safe; it looks good. I rub it on my lips. I turn on the tap and watch the water running, listen to its sound, feel the coolness of it splashing on my arms. When I can't take it anymore, I reach a cupped hand into the stream and scoop some out. It runs through my fingers and onto the floor. I go again but this time I push it into my mouth and swallow it. I try not to think about the evil bacteria, the viruses swimming down into my gut. I take another handful, then another. The life slowly seeps into me. It feels like rain after a long drought. I picture my withered insides returning to normal, soaking up liquid like a sponge.

With my brain cells watered, parts of last night swim up through my memory. I see Beck standing on the beach in the dark with the thunder of waves behind her. I rub water over my face and into my hair, washing away the bad thoughts. There is only one thing for all this confusion – surf.

It is breakfast time but hunger can wait, I am in bad need of salt-water therapy. On the beach, I pull on my rashie and reef boots, and carry my board around the curving reef to where the competition stand juts up in front of the break. It is little more than a bamboo hut built high above the water and how it puts up with the high-tide wildness of *Lakey Peak* is a mystery. Small pools dot the reef; they are full of marbled snail shells, sea snakes, feathery weed. Cloud reflections roll through them.

'Gurg! Wait, Gurg.' Niagara stumbles towards me in a pair of old brown socks. This is sharp rock and coral but he doesn't own bootees. He is wearing a 4-mill steamer and has an old foam shark biscuit tucked under his arm.

'I think you might be a bit overdressed, Niags,' I say as he winces his way over the reef.

'Borrowed the wetsuit,' he says. 'And the board.'

'Looks like a bit too much rubber,' I say. He is sweating badly and the suit has worn a red mark on his neck. I hate to think what it has done to his dragon bite.

Out at the *Peak*, it is breaking at about five foot. A booger gets sucked over the falls and worked badly by the next two in the set. He crawls out across the reef. There are huge marks raked on the bottom of his lid.

'Are you sure you want to go out, Niags?'

'Sure, Gurg. Looks awesome.'

'You surfed much before?'

'Plenty.'

He doesn't have any flippers and is going to have a bastard of a time paddling his esky lid without them.

We reach the water and I stand and watch the waves for a while. The left has a critical take-off but mellows slightly as it rips across the reef. There are about twenty guys on it. One of them drops down the face, does a quick pigdog charge, then cuts back for a last slower section before the wave dies in the channel. The next wave breaks exactly like the first, as if someone is printing copies in the take-off zone. The right is shorter and steeper but it shuts down at the end. There are only a couple of guys there. A rip is rifling around the impact zone and out in a big arc past the left.

Niagara has to shout over the powder blast of the waves. 'What're you waiting for, Gurg?'

He is gagging for a lesson. Nearby, another surfer is dragged over the falls. His board pops up in two pieces. He paddles furiously to get out of the zone but another wave drops on him. He surfaces. His left shoulder is open, the rashie torn away and blood streaming from the wound.

I drop my board onto the water and strap on my leggie.

Niagara shouts, 'Wait up, Gurg!'

No way. It's every man for himself out here. The rip is moving quickly and almost as soon as I hit it I am out the back with twenty other guys at *Lakey Peak*. The big bay sweeps past the bungalows and up to a huddle of steep mountains, thick with cloud. Seaweed gatherers are out on the reef.

'Can't believe I'm here,' I say to the guy next to me.

'First day?' He's a Pom with a boofy black 'fro jammed under a Gath hat.

'Yeah.'

'Been anywhere else?'

'Not surfing. Been in Indo over two weeks now, seen a few things. But no surf.'

He looks at me like I'm insane. 'What you come to Indonesia for then?'

'It's a long story,' I reply. I look below, through the warm, clear water, to big yellow fish circling the reef.

'Gurg!'

Shit, Niags made it out the back. I have to give him points for that. He tries to sit on his lid, rolls it, and is left upside-down in the line-up. His big brown socks have come untucked from his wettie and are hanging limp from his feet. He surfaces and spouts out a mouthful of water.

'Been a while, Gurg! Bit rusty.'

'You *know* that kook?' asks the Pom.

I shake my head. 'Never seen him before in my life.'

A set rolls in and Niagara drops-in on a local, bails and gets swept into the channel.

'What a prat,' says the Pom and I have to agree. I mean he's not really my mate. It's not like I owe him one or anything.

'Your wave!' shouts the Pom and I realise that I've jagged pole position on the biggest wave in the set. More by luck than anything else, I am sitting right on the button. Everyone else is too far inside and they're scraping to get over the big left. It's a good size. Maybe six foot. There is no way I am ready but I turn and paddle, feel the water rising and pushing. Jumping to my feet, I take a vertical drop, land and cut a smooth arc to the lip. I am on my forehand, the goofy-foot advantage. I gather speed and drive hard off the bottom. Then I see Niagara paddling like a huge floundering turtle on the steepening shoulder. I manage to pull high and push him away from my board but the wave sucks and buckles and takes us with it.

There is a lot of water here. Too much. There is not enough depth. When that happens it is like an explosion: water fires like gunpowder, boards break and bones splinter.

I hit the reef hard and the air leaves my lungs and rushes to the surface. The wave holds me there; pins me like a wrestler. I am drowning.

And they say time slows. And they say you see a light. And you walk towards it and you are calm. And I have heard that your whole life flashes before your eyes. And I wait for that to happen but it doesn't. There are no angels or devils or harps or fire. There is just a lot of water. And me.

I could have died. The cruellest thing of all – the knife-twisting bit – is that it was Niagara who saved me. And when I barked-up seawater and looked into his stupid, big dog eyes I wanted to kill him. He had dragged me up from the reef, pulled me through the impact zone and pumped the water out of me, but I still wanted to kill him. It was his fault, the shit-for-brains.

I have no lasting scars from my tangle with the reef – at least not ones you can see with the naked eye. I was lucky. Sort of. Something else I did that day was far riskier than surfing five to six footers at *Lakey's*. But it still had everything to do with water. When I drank from the tap in my room I knew it was the wrong thing to do. Mum knows best, they reckon. *Don't drink the water*.

I feel like I am going to die. My body is thick with fever, there are small armies roaming around my bed and I try to beat them flat with my palms. The faces of my friends are planets in tricky orbits above me. Beck is Venus – cool, dark, spinning into the corners of the room. Urs is Neptune, green and icy. And Niagara is Uranus, of course.

It is a hard stumble down the steps to our sunken bathroom. I have to squat over the hole-in-the-ground toilet while Urs holds me. I am so ashamed but too sick and weary to complain. My legs shake and my body throbs. The day is like a fireball scorching the splintery planks of our hut.

Then night drops and skin-lizards dance on the belly of the tin roof, darting at huge, soft moths that worship our forty-watt moon.

Urs goes for help. Her face washer is baked dry on my forehead. I have nothing left inside. I am too weak to sip water and when I do it leaves quickly from my burning arse. Urs returns with the bungalow owner. Her hair is swept up like a peaking wave and I scream at her, at her sea-black eyes and the hairy mole on her cheek but Niagara holds me to the bed and she pours something into my mouth and I know they are trying to kill me, and I try to fight them off but they hold me flat against the bed and the liquid burns my throat, so I close my mouth and it runs round my chin and settles in a sticky pond in the hollow in my neck. She cracks another bottle and forces my lips apart and I hear Beck crying. I shout, *I'm sorry, Beck! I'm sorry!* But she doesn't hear me because the night is going stupid and wild with cicadas, fat with their alarm sound and Belacan howls and starts off the pack-dogs outside and I smell something terrible burning, I am on fire, the bed is smouldering and bats smack into the walls.

I am dead.

But the next morning I am better.

Niagara says, 'Thought we were gonna lose you there, dude.' As he drizzles bottled water into the corner of my mouth.

The bungalow owner brings me rice. I eat a handful and it sticks like glue in my throat.

'Make you strong,' she says. Today she has lost her sea-monster look. Her hair is loose down her back and the mole has shrunk to a freckle. She leaves us alone.

'Where are Beck and Urs?' I ask. I am hanging to see Beck. I want to tell her about the planet thing, how she was Venus. I want to tell her I am sorry for saying I loved her.

'Um, Gurg . . . it's like this, man. Beck really wigged-out when you got sick. She left for Lombok and Urs followed her.'

I am gutted. I know what that means now – gutted. I really know. There is a huge gap inside me. It aches. I know it is not just the sickness.

I am too weak to surf so I sit on the hot coral sand and watch while others do. It is torture but it feels right. Maybe I am punishing myself for Beck leaving. Niagara brings me sweet tea and sits quietly beside me while I stare at the break, or the sand, or my toes. I walk along to *Nungas* and lie exhausted on the point, watching. It is small, only three foot or so and not breaking well. I wonder what Beck is doing right now. Is she staring out to sea?

Niagara finds me again. He has some local guy in tow.

'Gurg, you need to speak to this dude.' Niagara seems excited, a little breathless from the walk down the beach.

'Hi,' I say. I can't keep the boredom, the emptiness, from my voice.

The guy raises a hand and flops down on the sand beside me. I ignore him, keep staring out at *Nungas*.

'Gurg, this guy knows Castro!' says Niagara. 'He was here, Gurg. Your mate Castro was here!'

7 Child of the Sea

Gunung Rinjani, Lombok

We are on the track that leads from the village of Senaru to Pelangawan Satu – the First Gate into the volcanic crater of Gunung Rinjani. I feel as if I am stepping in Castro's footprints, my toes curling in my boots as leaf mould and mud works its way into my treads.

This morning, I checked every bungalow in Senaru but Castro has left no trace. The trekking guides know nothing of him and he didn't sign the climbing register. But the guy at *Lakey's* was sure he had come this way. I have to climb.

We stop for lunch after three hours of uphill struggle through the jungle. The monkeys drift from their trees to sit and watch us with their quick, clever eyes.

Niagara says, 'Cute little fellers, aren't they.' He offers one a biscuit and while it is creeping closer, its mates rush us from behind. For a moment the air is full of monkey screams as we grab sticks and scare them from our packs.

After the mayhem has ended, I spot our food bag hanging from a branch. 'They got our supplies, Niags. Your cute little monkeys.'

Niagara swipes at the air with his stick. 'Come here, you cute little monkeys!' he screams. 'Come to Uncle Niagara. I won't hurt you.'

But they sit high in their trees and raise their eyebrows as they eat our arrowroot biscuits. They crunch our noodles, shredding the packets until they float down like autumn leaves. Eventually Niagara gives up on his monkey war and we continue following the track up through the jungle.

After two more hours, we swing along a ridge and push above the cloud. To our right, Gunung Agung sits across a silver-plate sea, high over Bali. The triplets of Gili Air, Gili Meno and Gili Trawangan dot out from Lombok. We set up camp at two and a half thousand metres without fire or food.

In the morning we search for Segara Anak – Child of the Sea – the crater lake of Gunung Rinjani. But it is trapped like a pinned butterfly beneath a sheet of cloud. The new volcano of Gunung Baru rises from its shores, smouldering, threatening to blow.

My eyes are still wide for any signs of Castro. There is also a part of me that holds out hope that I will see Beck. She was heading for Lombok. I keep quiet about this with Niagara. He is sick of my crap.

'Boy meets girl,' he says. 'Boy loses girl. Boy gets a life, forgets about girl. Plenty more fish in the sea, Gurg.'

Good advice from Auntie Niags but I couldn't give a toss about fish. If it was fish I was after then I would trade our tent for a rod and head down to the lake to hook some.

The mist begins to burn off Segara Anak. It disappears from the edges first, a blue fringe appearing. Soon it is the colour of fibreglass resin. Today, we have to climb down to the lake and then around the shore and up to the second gate. Tomorrow, we will make the final climb in the early morning dark.

I am keen to get going but Niagara is brushing his teeth, farting around. It is like travelling with an old woman. I would be better off without him, much faster. Now I have slotted into travel mode I don't really need him around. He is an embarrassment and a pain in the arse. He is wearing a shirt with a Swiss flag on it. The dragon bite is uncovered, weepy and attracting flies.

Eventually, he shoulders his sack and follows me down the steep track. Belacan trots along beside us, sniffing the air and growling as if he doesn't trust the place. It is only half an hour down to the lake but the track is almost vertical and we have to climb over boulders and sheer rock faces. By the time I reach the water, I am hot and sweaty. Niagara is miles behind. He walks slowly, dawdles to check everything out. The man has no idea of pace.

There is a group of Swiss trekkers camped by a small stream. They are all over forty and have striped shirts and orange suntans. The men are wearing close-cropped beards, like it is some kind of uniform. Ski poles are propped-up against their dome tents, water bags are hanging from trees. These are the people that brought us the Swiss Army Knife.

I smile at them as I pass, walk over to the water and pull off my boots. I stand ankle-deep in the lake. It is cool. There are fishermen here balancing on rocks with their long bamboo poles held out over the water. They have carp, stringed through their gills and pegged to the bank. Even though it is mid-morning and warm, there is no one swimming. If this was Australia, it would be chockers.

I pull my shirt over my head and throw it towards my pack. One of the Swiss guys waves his striped arms at me. He looks upset but I haven't done anything to the dickhead.

I dive under the water. It is so cold it takes my breath away, but when I rise, it is to the sight of the new cone – Gunung Baru – and the rim of the old volcano rising up to the summit of Rinjani. I am swimming in the crater of a volcano. I laugh out loud.

I freestyle out further, take a mouthful of water and fountain it into the air. It catches the light and falls into the lake. I float on my back and look at the clouds, try to make out Beck's face in one that looks likely. A small black one winds in from the edge of the rim. As it comes, it grows and twists until it looks like a shark. It ploughs towards the sun and covers it. The temperature drops. I shiver and look at the shore. Niagara is standing there with one of the Swiss Adventure Team. I wonder how he has explained his shirt and his lack of Swissness.

'Gurg!' he shouts. 'Gurg!' And waves me in.

I start to swim to him. He keeps shouting, 'Gurg! Gurg!'

It is really cold now – freezing – and I feel like there is something beneath me, forked tongues wrapping round my toes, claws reaching up to prick my soft belly and legs. I am chopping the lake to froth.

'GURG!' Niagara is frantic now, jumping from one foot to the other. Belacan is barking.

I am powering towards the shore, choking on water. The fishermen have dropped their poles and are staring. Above, the cloud is thickening and I can feel electricity in the air as the lake turns to syrup, holds me, draws me backwards, tugging at my legs and arms. Niagara's mouth is open but his words are broken by waves that have sprung up from dead calm.

Glimpses of Niagara and the Swiss guys crowded on the muddy bank, waving, mouths like caves. My lungs burning, shoulders tearing and the thing is unfolding itself below me. Focus on the rim of the crater, claw my way towards it. Fingers not pushing enough water. Arms blurring, heart exploding.

Suddenly, my knees graze the bottom. Pulling myself to my feet, I wade through the sucking mud and away from the lake.

Niagara comes towards me, Belacan yapping at his heels.

'Gurg, you can't swim in there, man. It's bad.'

'Bub-bad?' I am shivering and it is hard to spit the word out.

Niags points behind him. 'That dude told me there is something bad in the water.'

The Swiss guy comes over and stands with his orange hands on his hips. 'Hello, yes, bad thing in the water. I don't know the English word for it but it is very tiny-small and gets into your liver. It can make you very sick. Better you don't drink or swim.'

'Wa-what about the fishermen? The fish?'

The fishermen have gone back to their poles and their strings of trapped carp.

The Swiss guy says, 'The liver-things die if they're cooked. Better for you if you don't cook your liver.'

Niagara cacks himself and slaps me hard on the back. 'Good one, dude,' he splutters. 'How do you want your liver done. Over easy? Poached?'

I kiss my middle finger and show him it. 'Piss off and die, idiot.'

As I dry myself off, I try not to think about my liver. The memory of the *Lakey's* water incident looms over me like a thunderhead. Niagara drinks tea with the Swiss Adventure Team and laughs a lot. They like his Swiss flag shirt and his stupid hessian sack. I am sure they are all laughing at me and my liver invaders.

We get on the track and make quick time around the lake and to the hot springs. From here we can see the Swiss team climbing to the First Gate, their ski poles balancing them like spindly legs.

Around the hot springs, piles of locals have set up camp – plastic sheets and tree branch tents, the smell of human shit and boiling noodles, clothes drying on the grass. Not a Swiss Army Knife anywhere.

We follow the stream down the hill to escape the crowd, weaving through the tarp shanties and staring campers. We end up at a steaming pond fed by a waterfall. The water must be okay; there is an old guy sitting up to his neck in it and brushing his teeth. We peel off our shirts and shoes and dive in.

The pool is warm and I feel it easing my sore shoulders and stiff legs. I do a couple of strokes over to the waterfall and let it drum my back for a while. Looking out from the fringe of falling water, I see Niags has joined the old guy on a rock in the centre of the pond. I wait for a moment before swimming over to them.

'Hey, Gurg. This is Jumadil. He's a Sasak. Tell him what you told me, Jumadil.'

I wonder what the hell a Sasak is, but Jumadil has started on his speech and I need to concentrate. His English is a little out of the ordinary.

'Here have pilgrim. Yoooknow pilgrim, yes? He come to here making offer in lake throw jewel many jewel sometime watch sometime ring. Gunung Rinjani sacred like Bali Agung many peoples climb but danger yes. Some peoples climb new gunung fall slippily into lake drown dead eat by fishes.' Jumadil smiles. He has brilliant white teeth, maybe something to with the toothbrush parked behind his right ear. 'Mountain veries impotent. Most impotent for Sasak Lombok peoples and seconds to Bali peoples. Gods lives on mountains. Humans lives under. Sometimes gods angry sometimes not. Depend on peoples. Peoples good then gods good. Peoples bad then . . .' He makes a flowering motion with his hands to show the explosion of a volcano. 'Seas all bad. Seas many many demon.' He pulls a demon face – bug eyes, open mouth. 'Seas very bad.'

Give me the sea any day, I say to myself as I think about the climb to the summit. Us like ants creeping up to meet the gods.

We finish our soak and make the final push to Pelangawan Dua – the second gate. The tent we hired has worked hard for too many trekkers. The zip doesn't work and the door flaps like a loose sail in the wind. Through it, I see snatches of couples hugging each other, dragging the last sickening rays from the sunset. I should go and tell them how quickly it could be over. To give it up now and save a lot of heartache.

Niagara looks up from Uncle Max's journal. 'Whassup, dude. Not thinking about Beck again?'

'Nuh,' I say and get quickly out of the tent before he starts up.

I climb above the camp and look down. There must be forty or fifty tents, their domes like ripe boils on the mountainside. Fires are beginning to glow and I smell food wafting up from open pots. Thanks to the cute little monkeys it is going to be a hungry night for us again. Cold too. I never expected that of Indo, not in a million years.

I unwrap my postcards, flip through them, then place them in order on the ground. Eleven breaks for eleven months, their lips ripping across the slowly fading blue. Roti, Sumba, Sumbawa, Lombok, Bali, Java, Sumatra? *Ulus, the Mentawais, G-land, Padang Padang, Ujung Genteng, Panaitan Island, Lagundri Bay, Desert Point, Scar Reef, the Hinako Islands, Nembrala*? Square-edged jigsaw pieces that must somehow form my map to Castro.

My head explodes. Thoughts shatter and twinkle over the cards, enter the dust and rocks. I always thought travel would make me happy but I am miserable. Back in Bajawa, Granny said I would find who I am not looking for. Instead I have lost what I never truly had – Beck. The last in a queue of deserters, behind Castro and my father.

A guitar starts up. The tired old chords of *Hotel California*. Why would anyone carry a guitar up this mountain? And why would they play that song? Then I see the porters fetching water, gathering wood, and realise that if you have the money you can get anything carried here.

Laughter ricochets of the rocks. It is the saddest sound

I have ever heard. The furthest away from home sound. It echoes inside me.

I climb down to the tent. Niagara is better than nothing.

All I can see is pinpricks of light moving upwards like fireflies snaking into the sky. My boots are full of pumice – light stone from the heart of the volcano – and it feels like I am walking on cheeseballs. We are over three thousand metres above sea level and my lungs are hanging for air. As usual, Niagara is far behind in the blue-black night.

I am ploughing through a stone wall. I am a ball of pain. I am a chain of sorrow leading to Sumbawa. I am questions. Why do they leave? And why do I follow? And why am I doing this?

I know Castro won't be waiting for me at the summit, cross-legged and crazy with the altitude. I know Beck won't be there either. But I keep plugging on, one foot at a time, counting out the steps. Each one I take is one I never have to take again.

The pumice gets thick and impossible and it is like walking through sand. People pass me as I rest and I pass people resting, crying, dry-reaching over the edge of the track where it plummets into the dark and to nothingness. It is like a dream with no sound except the crunching of stones and the sawing of my breath in my chest.

This is wrong and stupid, this human need to challenge mountains. Everest, K2, even Uluru – what is it all about?

What is so special about a summit? But there is something silent dragging me to the top of this volcano. The gods are there. But Castro is not and maybe he never was. I should turn around and slide to camp. My body is aching with cold and lack of oxygen. The beam from my torch is not strong enough to reach over the steep sides of this razorback track and into the dark pits below. I should turn around. But I am nearly there, I am sure of it.

Day begins to seep into the edge of the sky. A thin scar of light over Sumbawa. I keep walking, watching my boots hitting the river of pumice. My body doesn't belong to me anymore.

I clamber over a patch of rock, some boulders, and along a thin cliffside path worn smooth by the feet of thousands of trekkers. Ahead, I can see the group of people who have already made the summit. They are huddled together and are being whipped by the wind. A group of Indonesians have made small heaters from candles and plastic water bottles and are cupping them in their hands as they melt and shed too little heat.

I have only the final steps to go and they are the hardest. I want to sit down and rest but the group are calling me, waving at me to stand beside them. Pushing myself, I drag my body up to the tiny summit crammed with twenty others. They pat me on the shoulder and offer me milk biscuits. I look to my right, to Sumbawa from where I came, and on the left – Bali. Something drops down inside me and it all makes sense. Being on the top of a mountain lets you see the world from above. Allows you to map your life. There is magic here above the cloud and I could stretch and fly out over the Indian Ocean. The air is clean and the clouds are jellyfish shadows on the sea.

Then someone lights a cigarette and the breeze gets slicked with smoke. I look at my feet and see the cairns of biscuit wrappers and drink bottles. Leave only footprints, they say. And rubbish. And noise.

I feel sick and I'm sure if Castro walked this way he would have too. Suddenly I want to get away from all these people and their piles of Goretex and hiking boots. Down the track, a stream of weary trekkers struggles upwards.

On the Bali side of the summit is a tricky little ridge ending in a point of rock overlooking Segara Anak. I walk down and sit watching the triangular shadow of Rinjani reach over the sea and onto Bali. If this had been a year ago I would have run off a full roll of film and thought nothing of it. Now I am happy just to have it stored inside me.

I know why Castro would have come here, far from the surf spots of *Ekas* and *Desert Point*. He would have found somewhere quiet like this to sit and think. Watching and thinking were almost as important to Castro as surf. And he was always a planner, always one step ahead of the game.

Niagara's bellow breaks into my peace. 'Gurg! Gurg! We made it, man! Wooooohooooooooooo!' He is doing his spastic seagull dance over on the summit and I have to laugh.

I get up to leave and, as I do, I dislodge the rock I was

sitting on. It rolls down the slope, a smoky trail of dust reeling out behind it. Finally it drops over a cliff and towards the cone of Gunung Baru. Slapping my pants clean, I look at where it came from. More bloody junk – a film canister. This whole volcano is a rubbish dump. I pick up the canister and put it in my pocket, a token effort.

Together, Niagara and I return to Gate Two camp.

Maybe it was a waste of time to come here. I didn't find Castro and I didn't find Beck. I am crossing grasslands on the way home from Rinjani. We are headed to Sembalun on the far side of the mountain where we can catch a *bemo* to Senaru. The grass is shoulder height, and yellow. It hisses like a whisper as I pass through it. In the lowlands, the sun is a blowtorch. I can't believe this morning I was shivering on top of the world.

As normal, Niagara is about a day behind. He still has no idea of pace and has taken to whistling *Greensleeves* over and over. It is like travelling with Mr Whippy. We are better apart.

I am vaguing-out, just looking at my shadow running across the grass, when I hear a shout and a guy in a Backstreet Boys T-shirt jumps onto the track in front of me. I wave stupidly at him. Another guy leaps from the grass onto the track behind me. They have machetes and I don't think they are wearing balaclavas to protect themselves from the cold. I can't remember if I have read anything about this in my

Lonely Planet. Should I run or should I walk quietly away? I'm pretty sure that is what you do for snakes; is it the same for armed bandits? If these guys would give me a minute I could sneak my guidebook out and check but they seem eager to get on with it.

Forgetting about what I might or might-not-have read, I grab my pack and heave it at the guy in the Backstreet Boys shirt. As he is struggling to get up, I run over his chest and sprint like a bastard down the track. I run like my jocks are on fire, jumping logs and sliding down hills, through dry creeks and into a patch of forest.

It is while I am sitting waiting for my heart to slow down, that I realise what I just did. This morning I put all my traveller's cheques and my passport into my pack. All my clothes were in there too. Worst of all, I have lost the postcards from Castro, my only link to him. Even the first one – that maybe came from Jasper – was in the front pocket. The balaclava boys will toss them in the lake. I can see them being nibbled by curious fish and liver invaders as they sink with my dad's bandana. I have lost everything apart from my board and rashie. They are at our guesthouse.

Now I am stuffed. Without my passport it will be difficult to travel. Without money, it will be impossible. The best I can do is ring home and borrow the cash for a ticket to Melbourne. The thought of it lodges like a harpoon in my heart. Back to Torquay. On the dole or some shitty job. Cold water until February and onshore winds all winter.

I can't believe it is over like this, in one horrible moment of chance. It is too early to go home. I haven't got what I came for.

As I am sitting on a log in the forest – broke and passportless in Indonesia with only the promise of home to look forward to – I hear a familiar tune.

My music teacher in high school told me that Henry the Eighth wrote *Greensleeves* for one of his wives. I forget which wife it was. As I remember, Henry was a ruthless mongrel at the best of times. He killed some of his exes and locked up the rest. Then he wrote a tune so that every time you're stuck on hold or jammed with thirty sweaty shoppers in a lift you can have some background music for your boredom.

Greensleeves is a pile of crap. But it's also one of those annoying songs that locks like a virus into your brain and gets stuck on repeat for days on end. That is why it is Mr Whippy's theme song – kids never forget it, not even when they are all growed-up and should know better.

Niagara comes sweating and whistling into the trees with Belacan trotting by his side. His hair is gelled but gone droopy with the heat. He is tall and zitty and the best sight I have seen all day. *Greensleeves was my heart of joy* – it's the only line I know and so I growl it over and over as Niagara whistles his way closer.

'Gurgly Gurg! How hangs it, bro?'

'Not so good, Niags,' I reply from my log.

'Wassup?'

'Got robbed.'

'Robbed?'

'Yup.'

'Where?'

'On the track.'

'What they get?'

'Everything?'

'Passport?'

'Yup.'

'Traveller's cheques?'

'Yup.'

'Clothes?'

'Yup.'

Niagara whistles. Not *Greensleeves*, thankfully, just one long hollow note.

'Bad joss,' he says.

'What?'

'Bad joss losing all your gear. Whatcha going to do?'

'Dunno.'

'Go home.'

'Probably.'

Niagara sits beside me on the log. Belacan comes up and licks my fingers. I notice he is looking healthier these days.

'Real bad joss, dude. Bummer having to go home. Shit, I can't imagine having to do it.'

'Yeah, okay, okay.'

'Would your mom send you some cash?'

'Not to keep going. She'd spot me for the airfare but I reckon she'd want me to come home.'

'You could try.'

'My mum's no millionaire. I'd have to pay her back ASAP. Couldn't do that if I was on the road.'

'So what you need is a loan with longer payback terms?'

'Guess so.'

'I think the Bank of Niagara can accommodate you Mr Gurg.'

'No, Niags. Not you. I couldn't take money from you. How can you afford it?'

'Hey, Uncle Max left me a nice little wad. I got plenty of traveller's cheques, just got to get some cashed in Bali and we are on the road again. Together.'

I think about what that means – being in debt to Niagara. Indebted. Then I think about the cold Torquay water and the dole queue.

'Cool, man. Thanks,' I say.

'No probs, Gurg.'

We reach Sembalun and pick up a noisy *bemo*. The driver is playing Whitesnake – some tragic eighties rock band – and smoking kretek. He is wearing a sailor-boy hat and his dashboard is smothered in stickers. We wind up the road to Senaru and stop at our guesthouse. Niagara pays the driver and we go for a beer in the restaurant.

I feel something in my pocket, digging into me. I pull out the film canister and drop it on the table.

'What's that?' Niagara asks.

'A film canister, Einstein.'

He picks it up and shakes it, opens it and looks inside. He tweezers out a bit of paper and flattens it on the table. It is a business card from Tubes bar in Kuta. The waitress bring us two Bintangs, icy cold. Niagara pays and then turns the Tubes card over.

The birds stop singing and the dogs stop barking. There are no cars on the road. Someone kills the doof-doof on the stereo.

I spin the card around so it faces me. The handwriting is so familiar that tears burn in the corners of my eyes. I read it:

If you get this then it is the biggest coincidence on Earth. Forget that six degrees of separation shit, this is a full-on miracle. Meet me at Tubes on the 22nd. I'll be the one with a Bintang in my teeth.

Niagara shakes his head. 'Well, that means a whole pile of nothings.'

But it is a whole pile of somethings. Niagara hasn't studied that handwriting like I have. The long loops and dots veering off like crazy satellites. This card replaces the twelve I lost today.

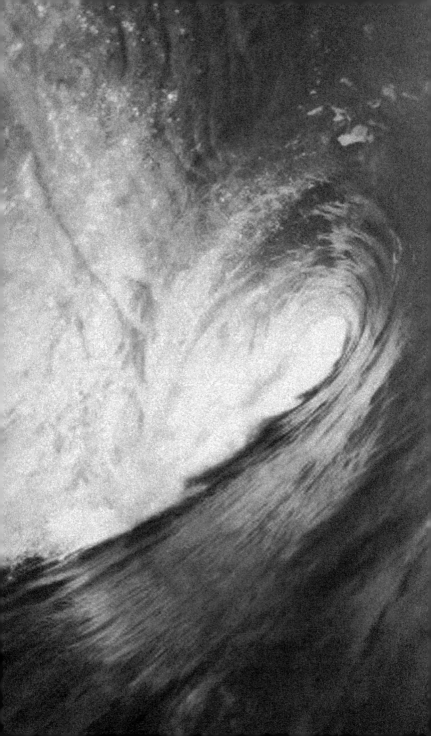

BALI
AND JAVA

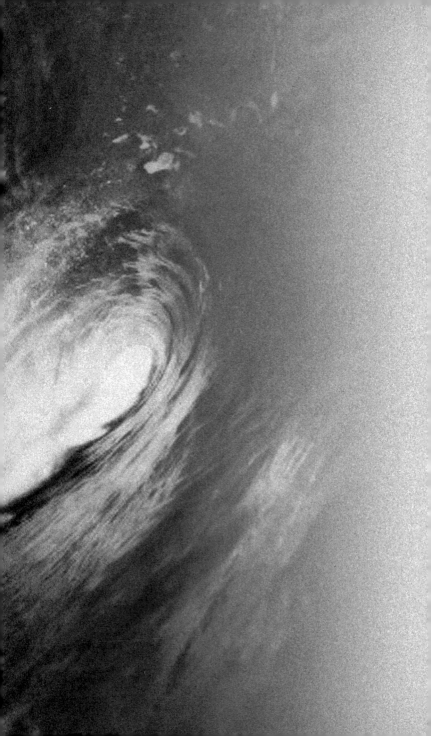

8 Kuta karma

Kuta Beach, Bali

There is a six-foot statue of Ronald McDonald opposite Kuta Beach. He is surfing in a very McDonald's way and wearing his stupid yellow, red and white suit. The bastard would be dragged straight to the bottom with those baggy pants and all that red hair. And it would serve him right.

I saw a doco once about how Kuta used to be this sleepy village. That is a long time gone. Today there are money-changers, watch-sellers, massagers, tour-touts, 'drink more piss' signs, armband tattoos. Anything here for a fistful of dirty rupiah: Foster's, VB, Live Dancing Surf Studs, Authentic Balinese Fiesta, Start Your Day Right Early Bird Special (2 pancakes, 2 eggs, 2 bacon), Live Sumo Wrestling, Internet (Fast Connection), ATMs, Pizza Hut, Rip Curl, Billabong.

A kid waves a local paper in my face. The front page screams, 'REBELS HIT SUMATRA!'

'I don't want it, mate,' I say.

'Maybe this?' He shows me a *Herald-Sun*, fresh off the plane from Melbourne. I try to take a peek at the footy scores.

'You buy,' he says snatching the paper away.

'How much?'

'Tweny-five, mite.'

'Forget it,' I say, continuing on down the street.

'Bloody Astrayun! All way bloody cheap, cheap!' he shouts after me.

I step over flowers and incense – offerings to demons or gods – as hawkers hassle me from the beach. 'Braid hair, mite?' 'Massage! Massage! Massage! Twenytousand!' 'Wan surf-board, mite?' 'Tattoo?' 'Marriwaanaaa?' The sun is a blowtorch and the Euro surfers with their yellowed-glass single fins have fire-engine backs and shoulders.

I am looking for a way out already and we only got here two hours ago. If it wasn't for Castro I wouldn't hang here at all. He'll be at Tubes tonight and I will be there drinking a cool Bintang at the bar when he walks in. We'll shoot some pool and it will be just like it always was.

But for now it is just Kuta and me. Niagara is having his toenails polished and I am stuck cruising this woeful scene. The beach breaks are rooted. There are about forty million sun-wrecked wannabes on each two-foot peak. They are getting hammered by the tiny shorebreak and dropping in on the locals. I see one guy take a big eat, his hire board flipping into the air. For a moment I catch 'Mr Snuff' in red paint on the bottom before it ploughs nose first into a bunch of Japanese swimmers. I keep on walking towards the Hard Rock Cafe; one eye on the water, the other on the prowling T-shirt sellers and wood-carving dudes.

Earlier, I tried to replace my traveller's cheques. Despite the TV ad where monkeys knock off a tourist's bag and in hours she is handed spanking new cheques by a smiling man from American Express, the wanker at the office said I needed cheque numbers, a police report, documentation. He told me how important it was to write down those numbers and store them somewhere safe, separately from the cheques. Cheers, mate.

Niagara gave me 100,000 rupiah this morning and told me no more until tomorrow. You can spend 100,000 here in an hour. Plus, I want to get over to Uluwatu and see if I can snare a wave. Taxis are 30 grand each way and everyone says there is no bus. I can hire a scooter for 30,000 but I will have to risk being pulled up by the cops for not having a licence. It's a hard call. If I spend 60,000 on a taxi that only leaves me 40,000 for food and beer tonight. If I spend 30,000 on a scooter and get done by the cops then I could get an on-the-spot fine of 50 grand. I'd be lucky to get a Bintang and a nasi goreng for 20,000 in Kuta.

'Hey, Johnny!' It's a cool-arse Balo in fake Ray Bans and a leather jacket. He isn't sweating. 'Wanna hire bike?'

The bike is an ancient Yamaha 125. The seat is cracked to shit and the exhaust is hanging off. 'How much?'

He smiles and I see his teeth are filed flat across the bottom. 'Fotty tousan for you, my fren.'

I keep walking.

'Wait! Johnny! Johnny! Tirty tousan okay.'

I return to him. 'Twenty.'

He jumps off the bike and leans it over to me. 'Twenny five, mite. Good price, you ask.'

It is a good price so I peel off a couple of tens and a five and we have a deal.

'Passpot?' He asks.

'Nuh.'

'Passpot!' He insists.

'I don't have one.'

'No bike.' He pulls the bike out of my hands and wheels it down the road.

'Wait! Mate!' I call after him. 'My money!'

He looks around and smiles his flat tooth smile and for a second I think he's going to jump on his bike with my dosh. But then he wheels the bike towards me. As he is handing me my money, I think of something.

'My passport is at my hotel. Give me a lift and I'll go get it.'

'No wurris, Johnny!'

'The name's Goog. You can call me that if you want to.'

'Ha, Goog, funny name. I am Wayan.'

He pockets the rupiah again and kick-starts the bike. I hop

on the back and we lurch into the traffic. Then we are rocketing down Jalan Pantai Kuta, too fast for all the hair-braiders and T-shirt hawkers to catch us.

I shout into the wind, 'Poppies Two!' Wayan nods, as he flies towards the winding laneway.

Niagara is out but I know what I am after and where he keeps it. He has sewn a flap into the inside of his pack and it is here that he hides all his valuables – his traveller's cheques, Uncle Max's diary and his passport. I fish for the passport and open it under the flouro light in our room. Niagara's big ugly head stares from the first page. Niagara Ulverstone Falls. *Ulverstone?* Could he get any weirder?

Wayan is waiting outside and I hand over Niagara's passport. Wayan looks at the photo and holds it beside my face.

'Merika, huh?' he says.

'My pop's American. I got a US passport.'

He pockets the passport and hands over the bike.

I am on the open road and heading to Uluwatu. My board is strapped to the rack and I am wearing boardies, a T-shirt and a pair of thongs. If I bail from this bike I will lose everything I own plus my skin.

There is a temple at Uluwatu, but I am off to worship the waves that rip across the reef at the foot of the cliff. Castro was mad for *Ulus*. He was always spouting off about it, had read everything there was written about the place. The only thing he had left to do was surf the break and I figure if he came through Bali – and if he *is* in Indo, he would have, for sure – then he would have gone for a wave at *Ulus*.

The Bukit Peninsula dangles like an apple on a string from the bottom of the island. It is the ball that the dog of Bali balances on. It is a swell magnet. Deep ocean juice hammers it and the sloping reefs shape the waves like master sculptors. There are a shitload of breaks here: *Nyang-Nyang*, *Green Ball*, *Bingin*, *Impossibles*, *Padang-Padang*. *Ulus* itself has *The Peak*, *Racetrack*, *Outside Corner*, *Temples* and *The Bombie*. I am thinking about all this wave choice as I hook a right off the highway and head down towards the ocean.

Before the steps were concreted-in, you had to climb down the sharp rock towards the sea. At high tide and on big days the waves break into the cave. Timing is everything at *Ulus*. But today the swell is small and I walk out of the cave and onto dry sand, blinking in the sun like a woken owl.

There is a drink-seller and a T-shirt hawker who can't even be bothered to stroll down the beach to meet me. Out in the water it is three to four and crisp as. There are about six guys on *Racetrack* and one at *The Peak*, which is not breaking well. Nothing else is firing. Pulling on my rashie, I dump my shirt on the rocks and walk towards *Racetrack*.

I make it through the shorey and paddle like a madman for the back. There is a good long lull and I am just about through when a set arrives. The guys start picking them off as I duckdive the first wave. The water is warm and full of foam and I surface to see a bigger wave arcing-up over the reef. I think I can make it over so I paddle hard. I watch it steepen. There is already a guy on it and I move quickly up the face behind him. Hitting the top, I relax and wait for drop down the other side. But the wave sucks and spits and I am pulled backwards over the falls and down to the coral below.

The water is full of light and bubbles and I catch the wild glint of the sun through it. I head upwards and break the surface in time for the next wave to break on top of me. I gulp some air, dive down and swim forward, reach the top, pull in my board and spit out a lungful of water. I stroke hard over the remaining two waves and I am out the back. It may be small but it still packs a punch.

I absorb some sun and salt for a moment. Let a few sets roll under me. There are six surfers out – a couple of shivering Balinese, two zinc-smeared blokes and a guy and a girl. The girl is on a booger and is wearing a fairly light-on bikini. The Balos are slapping each other and laughing, trying hard to get her attention, but she is well into her boyfriend.

'G'day,' says one of the zinc twins.

'How you going?'

'Good, mate. Yerself?'

'I'm great. How's it been?'

'Small the last few days but it's picking up. Later today or tomorrow'll be the time.'

His mate paddles into a three-footer and leaps into the crouch. His head bobs above the back of the wave as he fires down the line.

'Go, Dunger!' yells the guy beside me. 'Dunger and I have been staying up at Bingin. It was massive last week. The waves were slopping underneath the restaurant floorboards at dinner. We're off to Sumbawa tomorrow on a cruise.'

Those 'cruise' ships are moored off the coast at Lakey's. The guys are dropped at the break and picked up for pancakes and milkshakes after an hour in the water. A very cushy game. I keep quiet about having been there. I don't want to come off looking like a smart arse – like I am harder than these boys because I went overland instead of choosing the soft option. I nod over towards *The Peak*. 'Surfed that?' I ask.

'Got it good last Thursday, but there was a pile of guys on it. Plenty of hassling. Too much, mate. There's plenty of waves around, no point in worrying over a few with names.' He points his finger at the lone surfer rising and falling on the backs of waves. 'That guy is always on it when the swell picks up. It's like he's got a direct line to Huey. If he's out then maybe it's gonna to get better.'

'Who is he?' I ask.

'Some old Aussie hippie. Tried talking to him once but it wasn't worth the effort.' He shrugged the stiffness from his shoulders. Dunger paddles out again. 'Nice one, mate.'

'Wasn't bad,' says Dunger. He pushes his board underneath him and sits up. 'How you going?' he asks me.

The first guy says, 'Shit, where're me manners. This is . . . what's yer name?'

'Goog,' I say.

'Hey, Goog. I'm Benno and this is Dunger.'

'And that,' Dunger nods over to the girl on the esky lid, 'is one tasty little number.' Her boyfriend has scored a wave and is shooting fans of spray over the back.

'Hmm mmm,' agrees Benno. 'Brazil nuts, but. Worst bloody wave hogs in the world. Talk about drop-in merchants. "Don't mind if I do," they say and pick off all the primo waves leaving you with the shit. Don't even give the Balos respect and it's their bloody spot.'

'Yeah, but the chicks are *way* nice,' says Dunger.

'True thing,' agrees Benno and paddles for a wave. He is off, head-bobbing down the line.

The two Balinese guys get themselves a wave each. A sneaker-set gets up over the reef and I paddle for it. Out of the corner of my eye I can see the Brazilian chick pumping the water with her fins but she is far out on the shoulder. I feel the shunt and leap onto my board. The girl starts her drop in front of me and I am about to yell, *my wave*! when she pulls the whole shoulder down on me. I cut wide and try to get around the white water but it is no use. I fall into the wave, dive under and head to the line-up.

'See what you mean about the drop-in situation,' I say to Benno and Dunger.

'Brutal, eh,' says Dunger and paddles into one as the girl's boyfriend does the same. I hear Dunger shout, 'It's mine!' but the Brazilian is down the line and spraying rooster tails over Dunger. Dunger prones-out and catches the whitewater to the shore.

Benno says, 'Stuff this.' And paddles for an ankle-nipper, bodyboarding it up to the beach.

The Balinese catch a couple more each and then paddle in themselves. It is just me and the Brazilians now and I think the wave-to-surfer ratio is a bit better and I should get some action. But everything I paddle for, they are there. It pisses me off but I think, *Hey, I am at Ulus. The weather is perfect. The water is warm. Why get hassled?* So I cruise towards the lone guy at *The Peak*.

'What's happening?' I say when I get there.

He squints at me through his sun-crazed eyes, looks at me long and hard so I want to paddle in and get a mango juice and forget about talking to him. But I don't. 'Goog's the name,' I say and nod my head to make sure. He just stares at me, his eyes wicked coals, burning under salty eyebrows. He has an old blue tattoo on his forearm. His skin is leathery from the sun and there are nasty looking spots on his hands. Still, his eyes are fixed on me. I think about diving under and towing my board away so he can't see me and I can escape those eyes.

'From Torquay. Aren'cha?' he says with a voice like a pile of road grit in a drum.

'Yup.' How the hell did he know that?

'Not the first. Won't be the last.'

'What do you mean?' This guy is a hundred per cent whacko.

'Seen you guys come and go. Every morning, day-trippers from Kuta. Back before the sun goes down. Then home after two weeks of package tours, surfed yourself shitless on every poxy break between here and Sumba. I've seen a thousand like you.'

This guy is a bitter old fruitcake and I don't need his shit. I paddle to the Brazilians; at least they smiled as they snaked you.

'Castro was diff'rent!' he shouts at my wake.

The water drops twelve degrees. The sun goes icy. I feel like I have swallowed myself. I swing round to the old guy.

'How do you know that name?' I ask.

'Was a young fella, like you. Stayed with me a few weeks ago. Said he was going north. He was from Torquay.' The last word bounces off the cliff. The swell has dropped. There is no other noise. The Brazilians are eating bananas on the beach.

'Castro. What did he look like?'

'About the same as you. Longish hair. Pissy goatee. Good surfer. Loved his waves.'

'What did you talk about? Did he mention me?'

'He told me plenty.'

'Like what?'

'Like he hates sharks. Like he's never going home. Not ever.'

'What else?'

'D'you expect me to remember the whole damn conversation?'

'Do you remember where he was headed? When he was off?' He was going to Tubes tonight. I was only a few hours away from seeing him.

'North, I told you! He was going north. Maybe a week ago.'

'North? Where? Java? Sumatra?'

'I told him about a spot in Sumatra, said he might give that a bash.'

'Where is it?'

'Do you think I'm going to tell every bloody wet-behind-the-ears grommet that comes along about my secret spot? Do you think I'm mad?'

I do. I think he is out-there in a very major way but I need to know where Castro went. 'Look, this is important. Castro was my mate, *is* my mate, and I haven't talked to him for a long time. I need to see him, to get a message to him.'

'What's the message?' asks the man. He strokes salt water through his thin grey beard.

'None of your business.'

'If I saw him again I could pass it on.'

'Are you seeing him again?'

'Prob'ly not.'

This guy is driving me crazy. 'Just tell me where he was going. Please.'

The guy tilts his head and I think for a moment he is clearing his ears of water but then he starts whispering and I realise he is listening to something.

'Who are you talking to?' I ask him.

'None of your business,' he replies. 'I just want you to know it's against my better judgement but I can tell you where your friend was headed.'

'Good.'

He looks at me. 'But you must promise not to tell anyone else.'

'I promise.'

'Not anyone. No one. Ever!' He slaps the water hard and a cloud of spray rains down on me.

'I promise.'

'Pulau Badak.'

'Where?'

'Pulau Badak. Rhinoceros Island. Off the north-west coast of Sumatra. Very dangerous. Very secret. I went there in the seventies. Never again.' His eyes darken and lines appear on the bridge of his nose. 'There's trouble up there now. Some are calling it a war. Best you stay clear.'

I need to ask him for a map. Without a map or some decent directions I could be searching that sea forever. A freak set suddenly wells up over the reef. He strokes hard for the first wave and scores it.

I catch the second one and carve down the line until I am level with the cave. A barrel forms and I tuck tight inside it.

The tube begins to close, slowly like an eye. Then the day is winked-out and I am forced flat onto the sand. I roll and stretch and roll, then come up through the water like a chunk of foam. My shoulder is grazed but I can only think about the old guy. There is a crowd on the shore, a busload of tourists taking up the whole beach. The hawkers are hard at work but there is no sign of the old surfer. I paddle in.

I try to find Wayan in front of the Hard Rock Cafe. I ask the guy on the Hard Rock's door and he just laughs.

'Which Wayan?' he asks.

'Wayan. Wayan with a motorbike.'

'Four names for children born in Bali. Wayan – number one. Made – number two. Nyoman – number three. Ketut – number four. Then back to start. Many, many Wayan. Many, many motorbike.'

'This one had a leather jacket and sunglasses.'

The doorman thinks this is hilarious. He is cacking himself. 'Many jacket. Many sunglass. Heh-heheh-heh. Many, many Wayan. Girl too call Wayan – Ni Wayan. Boy – I Wayan.'

'Thanks for the lesson,' I say and push Wayan's bike down the beach road, looking for its owner.

The bike is cactus. It won't start no matter how much I kick it or swear at it. It is a piece of shit and if it wasn't for Niagara's passport I would push it into the sea as an offering. I am wheeling the bike along the pavement when a police car crawls past. I look up and the cop stares at me through his big mirror shades. He stops and gets out. Shit!

'Lie-sen!' he demands with his hand out.

I look at his hand and then at the bike. 'I'm not riding it,' I say.

'Lie-sen!' he demands again. His voice is full of boredom and a slight edge of you-can-do-this-the-hard-way-or-the-easy-way.

'No licence,' I say holding up the flats of my palms.

'Confiscate,' he says nodding to the bike.

'Yup.' I nod. It is not worth an on-the-spot fine on the slim chance that I might be able to find Wayan and trade his bike for Niagara's passport. I give up.

The cop's brow ridges up. 'Confiscate!' he shouts.

'Okay!' I shout and help him load it into the boot of his car. It doesn't fit well and he has to tie the lid shut with his belt. I watch as he drives down the beach road, eyeing me in his mirror.

Now it's just me and my board. Niagara is going to freak.

Niagara goes ballistic. 'You asshole, shitter, dumbass, assassassassassshitshitshit! Shit! Now whaddam I meant to do? What, Gurg? What were you thinking of, man! My passport! You already lost yours. D'you want me to be in the same stupidass situation as you? I cannot believe you did this to me, Gurg. After all I done. Dragged your carcass off the reef when you wiped out. Chased away your nightmares when you were stoopid enough to drink the water. Lent you money. Put up with your whiney crapola about Beck. Practically carried you all the way from Timor. You are the most self-centred asshole on the entire freakin planet.' He walks to the door.

'No, no, no! Not the planet. The universe!' He leaves, slamming the door behind him.

I sit on the bed. Me, the most self-centred asshole in the entire freakin universe. I have lost my dead friend, my passport, my mate's passport and my girlfriend. Home seems an impossible distance away. I try to force out some tears but they refuse to come.

We get drunk. It seems like the sensible thing to do. I say, 'It's my shout, Niagara.'

He says, 'It's my money, dumbass.' I can tell he has forgiven me but I am even further in his debt.

'What are we going to do without your passport to cash cheques?'

He says, 'Plastic.' And whips out an American Express Gold Card. 'Sir said "Only in an emergency" and I think this counts. But I'll have to go to Jakarta for a new passport.'

'And me?'

'You are coming with me, Gurg. This is your mess and we are going to fix it together.'

Looks like I'll be hitting him for a new passport for me too, but I'd better let that one simmer for a while.

We go to Tubes for dinner. The stereo is blaring distorted

cock-rock into the humid air. I know Castro isn't here but I ask at the bar anyway.

'Have you seen a guy in here? Long, messy hair, little goatee. A surfer.'

'Wha?'

'I am looking for a surfer,' I shout.

'Plenny surfer, mite. Look.' The barman points around the room using an empty glass. He's right – plenty surfers.

'He's called Castro. I'm meeting him here tonight.'

The barman shakes his head. 'You wan drink?'

'Yeah, two Bintangs.'

'Big? Small?'

I hand over the hundred thousand Niagara just gave me. 'Big. Besar!' I shout.

We eat burgers and chips and watch surf vids. There are heaps of girls here, white strap-marks on their raw shoulders and skimpy dresses. I try to forget Beck and Castro for one night. A movie comes on but the machine breaks so many times that we get bored and wander up the lane to Jalan Legian. Castro isn't turning up tonight. Maybe never.

After the backwaters of Lombok, Flores and Sumbawa everything is too bright and too loud. You can have an 'Arak-attack' for 20,000 and magic mushies by the secret glassful. There are Aussie pubs, cowboy bars, clubs in the shape of ships. We drink beers for three different happy hours and drift on.

By 3am everything is out of control. Pissed Aussies and Poms brawl on the street, shirts pulled up to show big back-job tatts and wicked burns. Guys hold their heads and chunder heavily into the gutter. Small-time dealers huddle in doorways over the cherry glow of their cigarettes. The night is gone.

We are walking down Jalan Legian, dodging pavement pizzas and sleeping dogs when something stops me dead.

I am sure it is her. She is getting into a taxi with a white ropehead-rasta. She is wearing a green dress, her arms are nut brown. He is holding the door open for her and she is giggling and touching his hair. I call out her name. 'Beck!'

Niagara is carrying Belacan. He puts him onto the pavement.

I shout again. 'Beck!'

She turns and I know she sees me. I feel like I am underwater, drowning. Sounds are muffled, everything is far away. 'Beck!'

She gets into the cab and Mr Ropehead follows her. I see her face, yellow with streetlight, framed in the window of the taxi.

'Gurg.'

I run after the cab.

'Gurg!'

The cab is moving slowly. There are too many dogs and drunks around to risk speed. I am in a new dream now, the one where my legs don't move quickly enough. I am running but I am standing still. I am the Roadrunner of Kuta, stuck still, burning holes in Jalan Legian while my girlfriend escapes with a dreadhead.

The taxi puts on a burst of speed and turns left into Jalan Pantai Kuta. They are headed out of Kuta, up to Ubud or down to the safe, clean resorts of Sanur.

'Gurg!'

The taxi merges with the dark, into the bank of fumes. It escapes behind a pile of building rubble and flashing beacons. Suddenly, there is nothing but me.

I feel a cold dampness in the palm of my hand. It is Belacan's nose. I look down and he is wagging his tail. His eyes are bright. There is nothing that looks more hopeful than a dog.

'Gurg,' Niagara jogs up. He is sweating buckets, his face a quilt of red blotches. 'Whaddar you doin, man?'

'I . . . I . . .' I feel like throwing my guts onto the street. I feel like breaking something. I want to scream. And cry. I want to tell Niagara that everyone leaves. No one hangs around for me.

'I saw Beck.'

'I don't think so, Gurg.'

'It was her.'

'Forget her, Gurg.'

'No.'

'Forget her. You're looking for Castro.'

'Stuff you, idiot. What are you looking for? Eh?'

Niagara stoops down and gathers up Belacan. He shrugs.

'Uncle Max?' I shake my head. 'Uncle Max is dead, Niags. He's dead.'

'I know,' says Niagara. He turns and lopes towards our guesthouse.

Shit. I have gone too far. 'Wait, Niags. I'm sorry, man.'

But there are some things that you can never suck back once you've said them.

9 Shadow play

12 November 1971
Java

NIGHTBUS TO NOWHERE

i am jungled-up
six feet of fear
and feral thought
cong bleeding tracefire
rip of leaves
thok thok thok
of bullet hitting rubber tree
i am fear fear fear

Niagara hands me this poem as we are eating at a truck stop
in the middle of Java. I am sure this should be breakfast but
there are scaly chicken parts and green beans on offer so

maybe it is dinnertime. I don't know what Uncle Max is on about. I shake my head and pass the book across the table. Niagara wipes a spot of grease from the cover and looks at the page again.

'It's about Vietnam,' he says. 'Uncle Max didn't say much but I think he had a hard time over there.'

Should I tell Niagara about my dad? Things have gone badly for me lately when I've opened my mouth at the wrong time.

'He was a good guy. You would've liked him, Gurg.'

I pick at the hard claw of my chicken foot, use it to stir my plate of rice.

'He said he was scared the whole time. His hands shook when he talked about it. Mom said Vietnam clicked some switch inside him so he could never be happy. Not properly. Didn't want a family. Said it would just spread the misery around.'

Belacan is curled at my feet. I drop my chicken foot on his rump. Tenderly, he grips it in his teeth.

'Best uncle you could ever wish for, though.'

Belacan crunches down on the chicken foot.

Everyone piles on the 'AC, VCD, recleaning seat Bus Malam Executive'. I climb the steps, each one a mountain between me and the impossibility of finding Castro, and settle into my broken, but recleaning, seat. We are still ten hours out from Yogya. After a couple of days there, we'll move on to Jakarta to fix our passport situation. I am sick of this journey.

Yogya arrives like every other town along the way. It sprawls along the highway like a bunch of boxes dropped from a passing truck. As we get closer to the centre, the boxes get closer and the traffic thicker until we are moving through a fog of bikes, cars, taxis and buses.

We pass a family on their way to early morning prayers. There are four of them on a 50cc scooter. The youngest, a boy of about four or five, is standing up in the platform between the seat and handlebars. None of them are wearing helmets and they smile and wave at our bus as we pass, even the dad, who has to loosen his grip of the bike with one hand. The scooter wobbles, hits a pothole and the hard shoulder, before snapping back to the tar.

I close my eyes and see my own family. My dad at the wheel of our old Valiant, its rag-top flapping as we cruise the road to Spout Creek. Priya and me arguing over comic books and seat space. Mum turning to give us her death-stare.

I catch my reflection in everything as I travel. The road has become a mirror.

It is eight in the morning when we book into the Hotel Dendam. Yogya is still yawning and scratching its belly under smoky skies.

Out on Jalan Malioboro the hawker stalls are setting up and starting to crowd the pavement. Rows of brightly painted *becaks* – cycle rickshaws – line the road, their owners sleeping with their feet on the handlebars.

A man with a whip-thin moustache and a double-breasted suit slips out of a doorway. 'Hello. Yessir. Hello.' We keep walking but Belacan grabs him by the trouser leg. The man shakes him free and follows us. 'Hello. My name Harry. Harry Pineapple.' He tries to push his face into ours but we are focussed on the search for breakfast.

'All the world likes pineapple. Hey!' He points with a thumb to my hair. 'Long hair – long life! I am studen of art. Wan to see my painting school? Batik. Very nice. Looking is free!'

'No thanks, Harry. We don't want it. We need breakfast,' says Niagara. He is wearing his Swiss flag T-shirt again. It may be smelly and dirty but Niags reckons it's the safest. No one picks on the Swiss. They may be famous for knives but they never use them.

'Brekfass? You wan brekfass?' Harry's eyes widen. 'I have brekfass. Egg boil, toas, noodle.'

'It's okay, thanks.'

'Banana, cornflek, kopi.'

'We're right, mate,' I say, holding my flat palm at him. This guy is a pain in the arse.

We reach a cross street and a boy leaps from behind a juice cart on the other side and starts shouting at Harry. He yells back and the boy lobs a starfruit at him. Harry ducks but the boy lets fly with another . . . and another, until Harry retreats to his side of the street. He stands on the other side swearing and picking starfruit skin from his hair but the boy just laughs.

We continue on and the boy comes with us. He is small, with a dirty neck and a grimy grey singlet that says MY AUNT WENT TO YOGYAKARTA AND ALL SHE BROUGHT ME BACK WAS THIS LOUSY T-SHIRT. His arms are covered with plasters. I can see the whirlpool of his hair swarming with lice.

'Hellosir. My name Tikus. Tikus is mouse. I am artis. Wantoosee my artis school. Come. This way.' He walks back the way we came but when he sees we aren't following, he quickly returns. 'Maybee toomorrow, yes? Today sight-a-see. I touris guide numberone Yogya. I take show you market, buy dog.'

I point at Belacan. 'We have a dog.'

'Too small. Not good eat. Big dog, froootbat, jungles cat. Mennies, mennies bird. Too mennies bird. Your short is rip.' He points at my travel-battered boardies. 'I show you cheap short. You go dandut – dirty dancing. You go disco – Borobodur Bar. I show you all. Taman Sari, Kraton, Prambanan, Borobodur. See fire mountain. Very danger. We go look at fire. Touch.' He mimes touching lava, very gently, with the tips of his dirty fingers.

We duck into a shopping plaza. The guards look at Tikus and grip their batons. He slinks off.

Inside, the plaza is all escalators and neon. Upstairs, we order toast, scrambled eggs and milkshakes. I feel like I have slipped home. It is too weird. Outside, Indonesia is rumbling by, but here in the air-conditioning it is a spring day in Torquay. Beautiful girls cruise the shops. Guys hang over the rails and shout into mobiles.

I slurp the bottom of my milkshake. 'You want another?' I ask Niagara. This is my code for, *I need some money.*

'No, thanks, Gurg. But, here, you have one.' He hands over a twenty. Money is served a dribble at a time.

I pay for my milkshake and get a voucher. At the drink counter, I feel a tug at my sleeve.

'Tikus, very like milkyshake.' Tikus must have dodged the guards and traced us.

'Here,' I say. 'Have this one.' I stroll to our table with Tikus in tow.

'Ah, Mr Tikus,' says Niagara. 'Long time, no see.'

Tikus guzzles the whole shake in one go. He winces and burps, holds his small stomach in his hands.

'Too much, eh?' Niagara says.

'*Manis*,' says Tikus, smiling and closing his eyes. 'Sweeeeeet.'

'You hurt?' I ask him, pulling at one of his plasters.

He pinches my finger until I let go. 'No. Nee-koteen this one. Patch. Impot oversea.'

Niagara's eyebrows point to his bloodshot eyes. 'Beg your pardon?'

'Stopischmoking. Patch Nee-koteen.'

I finally get it. 'Nicotine patches. He's trying to stop smoking.'

'No. Tikus not ischmoke. Patches is good. Brian from Yoo-Ess-Ay give to me.'

'Good old USA, eh.' I look at Niagara.

'First is Dacks from Perf, Orstray-yee-ar.'

Niagara nods at me.

'Then is Jenny, Yoo-Kay. Then Yuno, Swee-den. Then . . .'

'Okay, Tikus.' I hold up my hand. 'We don't need the whole history.'

'So Tikus guide. Small charge. One millions, one day.'

He aims high this boy, I'll give him that. 'We don't need a guide, Tikus. We're only here for a couple of days.'

'Okay, okay. One hundreds tousands, one day.'

'No, mate.' Niagara and I get up to leave.

'Okay two days same price. Cheap cheap.'

We shrug him off and head for the escalators. Behind us, Tikus grabs Belacan and screams. Turning, we see him run to the railing with the dog. He hangs him over the two-storey drop. Belacan squirms and licks his hands. We move very slowly and carefully towards him. I can see the hard glitter of floor tiles far below.

'I drop!' screams Tikus.

'Easy, mate,' I say.

'I drop!'

Niagara holds me. 'It's okay, Tikus,' he says.

'No. I drop dog.' He is almost crying. 'Tikus no rupiah, sleep street, no makan, hunger, mummydaddy dead.'

'It's okay, buddy,' says Niagara. 'We'll give you some money, some food. It's okay. Just put the dog down.' He moves towards Tikus with his hands up like he is surrendering.

'No. Stop! I drop dog. Drop!' He shakes Belacan over the polished steel rail. 'Drop.'

'Come on, mate. Take it easy,' I say. 'Put the dog down and we'll talk about it. You can be our guide. We'll pay you and feed you. First put Belacan down.'

Tikus smiles. He smiles big-time. His face cracks with it and the sun comes out over his brow. His eyes turn into little lumps of coal. He laughs.

'Belacan?' he says. 'Haha. Belacan!' He still has our little dog hung out over the tiles. A man is wheeling a display cart across the floor; he looks up. We are twenty feet above him, easy. Tikus's arms are shaking. 'Belacan! Smelly Belacan. Hoohoohoohoo!'

'Yup, that's the name I gave him,' says Niagara. 'And if you drop him then no rupiah.'

Tikus rocks his head from side to side. 'Belacan . . . Belacan . . . Belacan . . . Belacan . . .'

Niagara makes a lunge for Tikus. It scares him and he lets go.

A falling dog howls in a particular way. Once you have heard it you never forget.

Mum used to sing me a Joni Mitchell line when I was young and thought I hated her for one reason or another. She wanted me to see how you don't always care about what you have until it disappears from your life. This hits me while we are leaping down the first set of escalators. Belacan was our mascot. He was always there when we needed him with a wet nose and a well-timed tongue.

I prefer the Fauves; they sang *Dogs are the best people*. I am running through a forest of quotes for the next set of escalators. When I met Belacan he was a bag of scuzzy fur and bones but he grew on me.

We fly off the escalator and run to where Belacan fell.

There is a Teletubby display on the ground floor and its plastic-sheet roof has a neat dog-shaped hole in it. Belacan is worming his way from under a pile of linty creatures with TVs for bellies. He has Tinky Winky in his mouth and is looking pretty chirpy.

We hire Tikus anyway. Even though he is a ten-year-old nicotine-addicted hawker who dropped our dog twenty feet onto a Teletubby display, I think he has a good heart. Actually, Niagara agrees to hire him and that is fair enough as he has all the dosh.

We give our guide the afternoon off and he promises to take us to a *wayang kulit* show this evening. Niags is stoked. Uncle Max was a puppet master.

The air is like molasses – dark and warm – draining through the trees. Tikus has borrowed or stolen a *becak* and is pedalling us through the night. The only sounds are the whirring of spokes and Tikus's grunts as he swings the heavy cranks. I want to take over but Tikus is afraid of losing the good price he has negotiated for transport.

The bushes at the side of the road are pimpled with

fireflies. The moon is snuffed under cloud. We could be headed almost anywhere. Tikus takes a sharp left along a dirt track beside two tin shacks. It is even darker here; the path hung over with sharp branches.

Belacan pricks up his ears at the barking of dogs. Then we see light, glimpses at first, through the trees, and then flat patches spilling into the surrounding forest. As we approach, everything suddenly snaps into darkness.

'It's begin,' says Tikus and, jumping off the *becak*, runs down the track into a village. Niagara, Belacan and I follow, to the hong-hong of xylophones, gongs and strange drums.

There are about forty or fifty people here, crowded in front of a white cloth screen. Their faces are orange from lamplight and candles placed on wooden verandahs. Kids slump in their mothers' laps, grandmothers in sarongs sit cross-legged beside teenagers wearing death metal shirts. The sweet-sour breath of kerosene wafts in from the lamps, the candles sputter and drip wax. Tikus shoves some kids away and we sit down beside him. The ground is cool.

A shadow flickers across the screen. It flutters for a moment like a restless moth, then lands – a sharp profile of a human-like figure. Its nose is long and pointed, a headpiece rising like a wave from the top of its head. The lamp shines through the tiny holes stamped in its body. It is a lace person – half-human, half light.

In year eight photography, we arranged keys and coins on photo paper and exposed them to light. Their shapes turned bone white, the rest of the paper was drenched in black. The *wayang* on the screen is a negative of this memory.

Although the *dalang* is hidden by the screen, we can hear his chatter, the brittle static of his voice as he wafts the puppet across the screen. Another character arrives and there is a long period of talk. My shoulders and legs ache, small stones press into my skin. More characters, more talk. Tikus is so absorbed that I don't want to ask him what it means.

The candles burn low, then out. They are replaced. The kids fall asleep. Tikus's eyes are leaded with tiredness. Niagara's neck is bent forward so that his chin rests on his chest. He is snoring gently. Belacan is in his lap, safe from the quick snouts of the village dogs.

It has been hours or days. There is no way of marking time. The trees are whispering, raining small nuts over the village roofs. My body is paralysed from the waist down. There is a battle on screen. Much shouting. The music quickens. I am swirling through the dark images. My body is twitching with the sound of metal gongs.

I hold my eyes tight-shut then open them. I do it three more times. Cicadas in the trees scream and I feel it sharp in the bowl of my stomach. Swallowing the hot, damp air, I pull my gaze away from the screen, concentrate on the outlines of leaves against the sky. They become puppets too, dancing to the metal-pot music.

The ground is littered with bodies, they are sleeping or dead, I cannot tell. Still the music keeps coming, faster and faster. My heart is lurching like a drunk in my chest, my body humming, and holes of light shining through me. The lizard wrist of the man in front of me flashes a watch. Four o'clock. I try to count back to when we arrived but I can't remember if we have been here one day or two.

The night is as heavy as the sea. Fat beetles arrive, chopper into position above the screen as the music steepens and I am drowning in these shadows. The puppets batter themselves against the screen, against each other as I watch the long fingers of the *dalang*, his shadow, tweaking at their bodies, pulling them any way he wishes.

It slaps me hard: long fingers – Jasper. The man with the longest fingers. He was the *dalang* in *our* shadow play, the one Castro, Aldo and I acted out across the broad foot of Australia. We picked him up on the Great Ocean Road and he clung to us like a curse. I am certain he is behind Castro's death, or his disappearance.

There are two puppets on the screen and they could be me and Niagara or Uncle Max and Castro. Or Max and my father, in their separate wars, with the swirl of gunship propellers – dark, then light, dark, then light. The gongs blasting like mines. Agent Orange candles slipping tongues into the night. Cicada screams.

The *dalang* twists behind his screen. Offers his puppets to the light. Darkness chisels the village, tiger-stripes everything.

The music is unbearable – too fast, too loud. The puppets are ugly. Huge. They spew themselves over me. My head is rocking. My neck clicks. My spine is fused. The music. The puppets: Max, Dad, Castro, Niagara, Beck, me.

Suddenly it stops.

A rooster shouts for the morning. Dead people rise and walk to their huts. I shake Niagara.

'It's over,' I whisper to him.

10 The Goddess of the Southern Sea

Yogyakarta, Java

'Here, read this!' Niags is sweating gravy. His eyes look red, as if he's been face down in a swimming pool for too many hours.

I spin the piece of paper on the table with my fingertip. For a second I think it must be a page from Uncle Max's diary (isn't everything?) but it doesn't have lines and it hasn't been ripped from a book. It's slightly damp. I pick it up.

> 27 March 1982
> *The fear is the worst. Fear of the enemy, fear of the unknown.*
> *I am scared of the future, fearful of what I have become.*
> *I abandoned the two things that could have made me complete. Rosa said she'd come away with me, leave Arch, but it was all too complicated. How could we know the life we started would be the end of ours?*

Niagara is staring out at the *becaks* on Jalan Malioboro. Uncle Max's writing is like those Magic Eye drawings. If you cross your eyes and stare hard, sometimes a pattern appears. Other times you just say you get it so you don't look like an idiot. This time I have to know; it seems important to Niagara.

'I don't understand,' I say.

'Max always sent me presents and cards. But he didn't visit. I knew Sir didn't like him. His own brother and he hated his guts. Thought that was just Sir. He can be such an a-hole.' Niagara threads Belacan's ear through his finger; the dog looks up at him with his big, sad eyes.

'Who's Rosa?' I ask.

Niagara flinches like he's copped a poison dart between the eyes. He swallows, the knot of his Adam's apple running like a yo-yo up and down his neck.

'Rosa is short for Rosalita,' he continues. 'She was a Mexican girl who crossed the border with her family when she was sixteen. Seven of them crawling for hours on their damn bellies, riding in trucks and living on a handful of beans between them. Picking fruit through hot summers, freezing their asses off in winter. She used to tell me the story when I was a boy. Said I should be proud of where I came from. Said it was my history as much as it was hers.' Belacan yelps. Niagara has his ear pinched between his fingers. Surprised, he drops it like a hot coal.

His lips crackle as he rubs them. 'Rosa made it north and met this guy called Arch. Just a regular dude who worked hard

and put money away. Got married at Niagara Falls and had a
baby named Victoria the year after.'

I feel the slow grinding of the gears in my brain, the
kerchunk of a penny dropping.

'Vic's my sister. And Rosa, she's my mom, Gurg.'

I breathe out hard like I have been given a quick one in
the kidneys. 'Your Uncle Max and Rosa . . .'

'Yup.'

'Shit, dude.'

'It gets worse,' says Niagara. 'See this last line, the one
about the life they started ending theirs?'

'Yeah, I see it.'

'Look at this.' He slaps the notebook on the table. The
cover has been ripped and there is a footprint on top of the
shadow puppet. Niags turns the pages roughly, words
blurring, days peeling away, until he comes to the last page.
The cardboard lining on the inside of the back cover has been
torn open and there is a piece of paper sticking out. 'Go
ahead, have a look,' he says.

I pull the paper free of the cover and smooth it on the
table. Some orange juice seeps through and the words start
to run. I look at Niagara but he doesn't seem to care.

Dear Max,
I have called him Niagara even though he is
ours. He has your eyes. If you are leaving, we
have to make the best of things. Arch will provide

for us all. He is a good man and I have hurt him
badly . . .

The orange juice has attacked the rest. I can make out the odd word, but it seems too private for me to read on.

I don't know what to say, but I know I have to try. 'So I guess you have a few questions for Uncle Max.'

'He wasn't my Uncle, Gurg!' Niagara slams his hand down on the table.

'Calm down, man,' I say, looking around. 'You'll get arrested or something.'

'Who cares,' says Niagara, laying his forehead softly on the table.

I should tell him that I care. That I do actually care about what happens to him. That despite all the stupid shit he has done and how annoying he is, I have grown to like this bloke. He is a septic tank – a Yank. He's a kook, a woeful dancer, a sorry drunk, a daggy dresser, a hopeless numbnuts. He is all of that and more, but he's my mate.

'I'm leaving, Gurg,' he says.

'No you're not,' I say in a panic.

'I am. It's over. This whole trip has been a joke. I've been following the trail of a guy who isn't what I thought he was.'

'But he is *more* than you thought he was, Niags.'

'More *and* less.'

'But don't you want to find him?'

'He's dead, remember. Locust Grove, Oklahoma.'

'Do you know that for sure?'

'The British guy, the one who knew Max from Asia – he told me Max was dead.'

'How do you know he was telling you the truth?'

'Why would he lie, Gurg?'

'Niags, you don't know for certain Max is dead. Death is only a word and unless you see it with your own eyes you can't be sure it's real.'

'You said it that night in Kuta, Gurg. Max is gone. My journey is over.'

I have nothing else to say that will change his decision. His mind is made up. 'What will you do?'

'I'll go home. Back to my job in the grocery store.'

'You going to be okay?'

He smiles. 'Ole Niags'll be just fine.'

'Can I write to you?'

'Tell you what – I'll write to you. If I give you my address, you'll only lose it.'

I laugh and know it's true. I write my address in block letters on a napkin. It looks foreign sitting there, small and far away.

Our road has finally fractured – split in two – and there is no way of cementing it together again.

'Tikus has got an idea of how to find Castro,' I say.

'You told Tikus about Castro?'

'Why not, what have I got to lose?'

'Nothing, I guess. So what's his brilliant idea?'

I shift on my seat, it has become hard and hot. 'We are going to Parangtritus to ask some sea goddess where he is.'

'Man, have you lost your freakin mind! You've let a ten-year-old snake-oil salesman bluff you that a sea goddess can help you find your dead friend. Are you serious?'

He has a point. I am limping between shreds of evidence. The trail winds like a dribble of stones, of breadcrumbs, all the way to Timor. But there is nothing even that solid about it. It may as well be smoke. The Tubes business card is gone. Someone on the night bus from Bali went through my pockets when I was sleeping. It would have meant nothing to them but it was everything to me. It was my only hard piece of evidence.

Maybe, if I can con a little cash out of Niags, I should just shoot through to Sumatra and try Nias or the Mentawais – places that Castro would surf. Or I could go to Jakarta, get a new passport and head home. But there is something nagging at me, telling me to take this crazy punt on Tikus and his goddess.

'I gotta try, Niags. It's a long shot but I gotta give it a go,' I say.

'It's a nowhere-shot,' says Niagara. 'But you do gotta try.' He drops a plastic bag and a big wad of rupes on the table. 'A present for you, Gurg. Good luck.'

'You should come,' I say, but it is only politeness. It goes unnoticed, like the bless-you when someone sneezes.

Niagara grabs his sacks and looks down at Belacan. 'You want him?' he asks me.

'I can't, man. He's your dog. He loves you, look at him.'
Belacan is staring up at Niags like he is some kind of god.

'I only got him to mimic what Max had done. He's Max's, not mine.'

'That's where you're wrong, mate. He started out as Max's dog but he became yours. You keep him. It'll remind you of our trip.'

Niagara takes Belacan's small snout in his hand and stares into his eyes. 'I guess,' he says. He loops a piece of rough twine through Belacan's collar, then holds out his hand for me to shake. I take it and pull him round the table and hug him hard against me. It's not possible that he has grown on this trip, but he seems taller than he should be. His shoulder flattens my nose.

'Come on, Belacan,' he says to his dog, and with that, he leaves.

They merge with the foot traffic on Jalan Malioboro – the artists, the hat salesmen, the T-shirt boys. He jumps into a *becak* and gets pedalled towards the Kraton. He yells to me, 'Watch out for that sea goddess. Bet she's a mean momma!' I smile and wave until I can no longer see the badly built nest of his gelled hair, until he is the faintest smudge in a river of colour.

On the street, tourists glide by, their skins shining in the mid-morning sun. Batik touts snake behind them, tugging at their elbows and tightly zipped daypacks. Couples point from *becaks* at ring-tailed dogs and rag-arsed kids. I am alone.

Now I am pared to nothing. Nothing to lose. Nowhere to go but forward.

I empty the bag he left on the table. A new pair of shorts – brilliant green with a swirling eye on the pocket. I try to laugh but it comes out all wrong, halfway between a sob and a sigh.

This is where the Goddess of the Southern Sea hangs out; this wave-shattered coast with teeth of volcanic rock chewing its edges. We are kicking through dark sand and blackened driftwood to the Samudra Beach Hotel at Parangtritus. The Goddess has a suite there – room 319 – a shrine for fishermen and sultans. Tikus is silent, sulking. I refused to buy him patches this morning and his body is dangerously low on nicotine. Scuffing his feet through the sand, he mutters long phrases of Javanese at the sea. He is a moody little bastard, but I like him.

At the hotel, Tikus takes a fistful of my dirty banknotes to the doorman. He stashes my board in a broom closet and we all sneak past the front desk and up the stairs.

'Twenny minit only,' says the doorman, unlocking room 319. Then, looking around nervously, he bends his way down the stairs.

Inside, there is a double bed draped with green and silver sheets. Paintings line the walls. I am surprised the Goddess doesn't demand five-star luxury.

'She is very beauty, yes,' says Tikus. 'First half month she is like this.' He points to a painting – long black hair, dark eyes and curves rolling into a foaming sea. 'Next half she is uglies.

Very, very uglies.' He pulls his eyelids down with his pointy little fingers and opens his mouth.

'What now?' I ask.

'Offer dress,' says Tikus.

I up-end my plastic bag and the dress I bought in Yogya falls onto the floor. It is green – her favourite colour. I place it carefully in front of her picture like Tikus told me. 'And now?' I ask.

'Now bed. Sleep.'

'In twenty minutes?'

'Try.' Tikus sounds like my mum when I was six.

The sheets are as slick as seaweed. I close my eyes.

'Think of Nyai Loro Kidul,' says Tikus.

'Nyee who?'

'Goddess! Think of her. And sleep.'

I try to let the Goddess into my mind but Beck keeps coasting by. I wonder what she is doing now, where she is. I think of her on Pulau Komodo, swimming to the coral heads. The night we slept on the bare boards of the pier, water slapping against the posts, clouds shifting across the moon. I think of Lakey Beach when I told her I loved her. Idiot! I screw my eyes tight.

'Sleep?' asks Tikus.

'No. No sleep, Tikus. Nothing.'

'Sleep! Hurry.'

Focus. Focus. The Goddess of the Southern Sea, feared by fishermen, half troll, half supermodel. Apart from a few paintings and what Tikus has told me, I know nothing about this chick. I drift towards Castro instead; it is him that I want to ask her about.

✷ ✷ ✷ ✷ ✷

'Come on, Googsy!'

We have paddled out beyond the break. We are only ten and the shore seems a long way off. I am following the soles of Castro's feet across the water; they are crossed over and I cross mine too because it looks cool and I want to be like Castro. The cliffs are dotted with cars. Lines of black ants, people, are crawling down the steps in the corner. It is summer and everyone is here. It's the holidays. Mum says Dad will be home soon. Definitely. He has just moved to Queensland to work for a while. Why did he take his box of secret photos, the army ones? 'He'll be back,' says Mum, and I trust her. Castro is getting too far ahead. 'Castro,' I shout but he doesn't stop. My arms are tired. This is a stupid idea. This is Castro's idea. 'Let's paddle out to the horizon, Googsy,' he says even though we both know it can't be done. Like getting to the end of a rainbow or something. His feet are too far away and I am tired. There are birds out here. Small terns. My dad watches birds with binoculars and so do I. The terns are fishing for sprats. They are silver, like bits of tin foil in the sun. Castro is far away. 'Castro!' I shout. He laughs. 'Come on, Snailman!' he shouts. His board is way heavier than mine, but he is stronger. And he knows it. He should slow down and let me catch up.

I can see down to *Boobs* and *Winki* and further to *Bells Bowl* and *Rincon*. It is a hot day. Thirty-eight, and not much swell. That is why we are out here instead of catching waves. Dad is going to buy me a board. A new one. He will probably bring one from Queensland. They have wicked boards up there. 'Castro! Don't be a mongrel!' I stop paddling. I am tired. My arms hurt and we are too far from shore. A big orange ship is out at sea. It looks closer than the beach. I feel sick, scared. I want to turn round but I don't want to paddle in by myself. 'Castro! I'm going in.' He doesn't care. He keeps paddling like a paddling robot and I am getting left behind. I turn my board around. Stuff him. I can go in to shore by myself. It is only that I am scared and Dad says fear is not even there, it's not real. Was that a shark? Just some seaweed. I paddle. I focus on the shore, at the cliffs with ants and cars. Mum is on shore with Priya. She will be reading *Woman's Day* and Priya will be building sandcastles. I want to be there. Not here. The shore doesn't seem to be getting closer. I am too tired. If I put my head down on my board the sea sounds like it is knocking on a door.

The rescue boat picks me up. I want to be sick. They give me water and cover me with a towel.

'My friend's out there,' I tell them and we go further out, looking for Castro. He has gone. Vanished like a puff of smoke.

'Maybe he went home,' says the lifesaver. He has yellow zinc cream over his big nose and he smells of beer.

'No! He's out there,' I say, and I try not to cry. I try not to. We go in anyway. Back to shore and to Mum and Priya. And Mum hugs me and cries and Priya sulks because I'm getting attention, not her, the baby.

And then Castro walks up the beach with his big fat board.

'What's up, Goog?' he says.

'Where were you?' I say.

'Paddled in,' he says. I want to hit him, but I smile instead. I can't be mad at Castro, that's just the way he is.

✳ ✳ ✳ ✳ ✳

'Sleeping?' Tikus's annoying whine hauls me to the surface.

'I was until you woke me.'

'Dream of fren?'

I don't want to tell him about the dream – it didn't mean anything. 'No go, Tikus. Your Goddess is bogus.'

'Okay,' says Tikus, grabbing the dress from in front of the painting. 'We try sea.'

The sea is a frenzy of foam and bad angles. Waves are battering their heads on each other, spinning up into the wind. The water is grey and white, the colour of boredom and death. I am standing like an Easter Island statue on the sharp volcanic sand. I have the green dress in my hand.

I pull the ugly-arse shorts Niagara gave me out of my bag, and loop the dress over my shoulder. Then, shedding my old boardies like a snakeskin, I wriggle into the bright green ones.

They are way lairy but I figure I may as well give them a go; plus I'll need something dry to change into.

'No. No those shorts!' shouts Tikus. His words are tackled hard by the wind and bundled into the Indian Ocean.

'What's wrong with them?' But I know there are a hundred things wrong with these shorts.

'Bad. Bad colour, Goog.'

'What's wrong with this colour? This is the Goddess's favourite.'

'Yar. Take you down. Marry wid you.'

'Cool.' I reckon I could handle a bit of that action.

'You like under water, Goog? You breathes water? No! You breathes air, Goog. You die!'

'I'm not going to die, Tikus. Here, give me my board. I'll go out and drop this offering out the back and that will be it.'

'No, Goog. Bad. I feel bad. You die. Then what about Tikus.'

'Here,' I say, handing my wad of remaining rupiah to him and grabbing my board. 'If I die, then you can keep the money.'

He brightens a little with the soft promise of cash between his fingers. 'Care, Goog. Be care.'

'I'll be very careful, Tikus,' I say and run into the shorey.

I only have to paddle out a little way. Just enough so the dress doesn't get dragged back to the beach. Tikus is watching me. He stays away from the water, as if it is acid. It terrifies him. I guess if I had been fed a diet of horror stories about the ocean then it would scare me too.

I stroke over a few waves. It is breaking all over the place. Pure chaos. I spot a channel and paddle hard for it. There is a fair rip running and, before I know it, I am fifty metres from shore . . . then seventy-five. I try to paddle across but there are towers of water around me. There is no way I would normally go out on a day like this. No way.

About a hundred metres offshore, I escape the rip. The dress is still looped over my shoulder and each time I duckdive, it washes into my face. I decide to ditch it and catch one of the beasts to shore. As I pull it from my shoulder, I glance over and see a wave building. It looks big; even at a distance it looks real big. It is swollen and dangerous, dark black at its heart and feathering grey at the lip.

I think about duckdiving it or at least swimming down so I can escape the worst. But it is too big, too nasty, for that. I turn and paddle. If it breaks with me then I have a chance at catching it to shore.

The wave pitches. It cracks and sucks air from around it. I can hear it – feel it – barrelling behind me. I am late on the take-off. Way too late.

I drop vertically, the nose of my board getting too much air. I land somewhere near the base of the wave, tail first so my board dips under like an oar. I fall backwards, my shoulder ploughing in, followed by my body.

It is quiet for a moment. Then the world erupts.

I am wearing green – the colour of the Goddess.

The beach is glasspaper on my calves. The sky is the colour of last season's oranges. I am 90 per cent fresh water and 5 per cent seawater. I am soaked in brine. Salty as an anchovy.

The face that rises over me is like rusted iron. It has black holes for eyes and wire wool hair. Ten-to-one I am dead.

Fifty-to-one.

Ironface smiles. He has fisherman's hands, the smell of the sea on them and bright scales for fingernails. I wonder where I am.

My shorts are missing, my balls shrivelled to nothing, my toes blue. But I am still attached to my board. It is slopping in the shorebreak. Someone should cut the cord and let it live its own life. Send it back to sea.

Villagers run down the beach in their bright sarongs and battered hats. They stand in a circle and stare at what the fisherman has dragged from the ocean. '*Ombak besar*,' they mutter. Big waves. They shake their heads.

I am getting stronger. The roof of this hut has twenty-five twisted rafters and a rusting patch of tin that looks like Belacan. The walls are soft palm wood. Rough windows are cut halfway up, shutters flapped open on the white afternoon. I am eating green beans and rice and shitting into a can. I am wearing a worn sarong.

My head spins when I get up. I hold onto the ladder-backed chair – the only piece of furniture I have seen here. I have trouble walking. Ironface follows me to the ocean, as if I am a merman and he is worried I will escape into water.

I stumble onto the beach. The ocean is a sheet of glass today. A mirror for the sky to admire its clouds in. I wish for Beck, her cool arms. I look at the polished sea and wish for Castro. I hug my arms to my chest and feel home drawing me back.

This trip is over. I have no money, no clothes, no friends, no leads left to follow. It is time to return to Oz. *Don't forget the way home.* I try to figure out how. If I paddle to the horizon I could snare a ride on a passing boat. What would be my chances of escaping months, or years, in a refugee camp in the desert when I hit Australia? My passport is gone. I have lost who I am. No one knows me.

I wander down the beach and flip rocks into the water. Some of them float – pumice – filled with too much air to be a proper stone.

In the village, a dog sings a mournful song. It is watching me from the bottom of some crooked steps. The village is like a fish trap – two rows leading at right angles to the beach, blocked at the end by Ironface's hut. It captures the ocean breeze, the salt-heavy air, feathers from seabirds, light chunks of flotsam. Me. The huts face each other, shunning the sea. The sea is cursed. It is boiling with demons.

Chickens peck the dirt, wander in bandy-legged gangs

between the tarps of drying anchovies. When they steal fish, the children are quick with a stone or a stick. The stragglers cruise the high-tide mark, feeding on sand fleas under the rotting piles of seaweed. A bird with a crumpled crest pulls at something green – a piece of cloth. It draws it out like a fish skin. The colour is so familiar.

I shoo the chicken away and it clucks like a hollow door being knocked. The cloth is at my feet and I turn it over slowly with my toes. They are my green shorts – the ones Niags gave me. Picking them up, I wave them at Ironface, and he smiles back at me like I am mad.

There is something bulky in the pocket. Something I didn't notice when Tikus and I were on the wind-hammered beach. It's a film canister, like the one I found on Gunung Rinjani. The one with Castro's message.

At least I have something to go home with, some sort of proof that this actually happened. I flip open the lid and find, instead of Castro's note, a sheet of paper. It is so tightly wedged that I have trouble getting it out.

It is a page of Uncle Max's diary. Another parting gift from Niagara. Another bloody quote:

'Now when I was a little chap I had a passion for maps. I would look for hours at South America, or Africa, or Australia, and lose myself in all the glories of exploration. At that time there were so many blank spaces on the Earth, and when I saw one that looked particularly inviting on a map

(but they all look like that) I would put my finger on it and
say, when I grow up I will go there.
Joseph Conrad, *Heart of Darkness.*'

That's just great, Niags. More shit from Uncle Max's sack of useless crap. But when I turn the paper over, I get a glimpse of something better.

In my hut, the door shut against Ironface – even though it is *his* hut and I am sure I am breaking every rule of being a polite guest – I study the map. I press it flat against the rough floorboards so that the impressions of knots and eyes swell between islands like vaccination scars.

It is a chart of North Sumatra. The port of Singkil on the coast. The wild Mentawais and Pulau Nias are sketched in a sea of white. At the top left of the page is the Banyak Archipelago and – nearly dropping off the paper, half ripped at the staple mark – Pulau Badak.

This is the place the whacko at *Ulus* talked about. He said Castro was going there. Pulau Badak – Rhinoceros Island.

SUMATRA

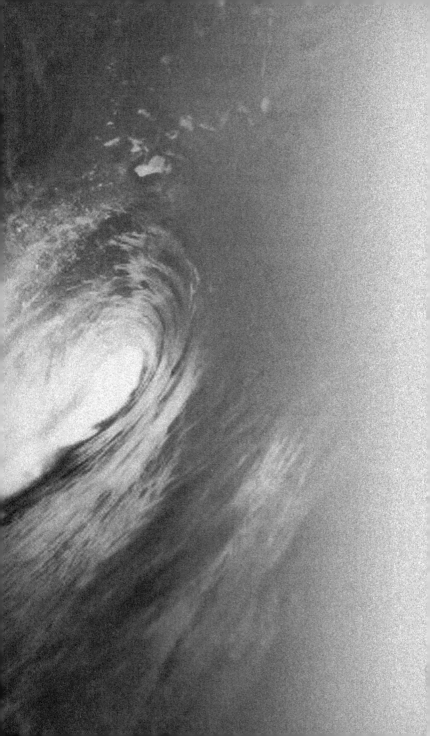

11 The sea and the stars

Ironface has brought me to a village by a deep river where a skipper and his crew of dangerous misfits have anchored their boat. They must owe Ironface a favour because, when he shows them my map, they nod and slap me hard on the back. The skipper offers me a swig of cloudy arak from a plastic bottle to seal the deal and by high tide we are motoring from the river mouth to the open sea.

The *Perompak* is an old fishing boat – fifty foot of rusting steel and wood. She has no nets. The big arms that would haul them from the sea are empty, the rollers seized. A motor thuds away below decks, thick smoke gushing from the boat's stern. One of the crew climbs up from the engine room. His arms are sleeved with grease to the elbows. His face is black with soot and oil, ringed around the eyes like a negative panda. I hope he knows his job and that his machinery will carry us where we are going.

Night drops like an axe and the ocean becomes a dark slick around our boat. The skipper refuses to use his lights, following stars across a waveless ocean. Stars so brilliant and countless they trick the sea into believing it is the sky. His crew, crosslegged in orange pools of lamplight, drag handfuls of sticky rice from a sheet of newspaper and fold them into their twisted mouths.

I lean against a pile of limp rope and wish myself somewhere else.

Castro would have hit all the surf spots through Java – *G-land, Ombak Tujoh, Cimaja* – until shooting out from Sumatra to Pulau Badak. I have missed out on plenty of waves but I am getting closer to Castro, I can feel it. After Sumatra there is only the long trek south or a flight north to the coral and bullets of Sri Lanka. He's definitely on Pulau Badak.

I miss not having him around. Miss the way we always knew what each other was thinking. Or thought we did. We were alike in so many ways. My old man up-and-left when I was ten, his mum died when he was three. We were both short a parent.

Castro's dad is a truckie who does the interstate runs. In his time away from the road, he breeds lorikeets. Birds as bright as twists of lolly papers. He knocked together an aviary from old pallets and chook wire. 'Good with his hands,' Mum called it. Those hands are the size of hub caps, scarred from years of rebuilding gearboxes and changing tyres. They are as strong as monkey wrenches but he can hold a newborn chick with the lightest touch. He's a good bloke, Mr Fidle. Not a complicated man, not showy or tough. Just steady, like a summer northerly.

We were always trying to get my mum and his dad together. Stupid kid dreams. Castro and me under one roof would have been too much for anyone.

Besides, Mum was never interested in anything long-term. She had a few boyfriends but Dad broke something important. She always kept something back after that.

Dad left a note on the kitchen table. Mum wouldn't let me read it but I snuck the odd bit – 'sorry', 'too late', 'wrong'. Those words were maggots, chewing at me for years.

My sister, Priya, and I cried. Priya soaked her sheets with tears every night. For six months, Mum kept us going with the story that he had gone to Queensland to work and would be home soon. But even Priya figured it out eventually. You never get over shit like that.

And here I am on a boat in the middle of the Indian Ocean. If I could trace my being here to one point, would it be then – the day my dad left? If Dad had been around, would my life have been better? Would he have kept me at home? How big do you make the map of your life? How much should you blame one thing on another?

The crew breaks out a pack of cards and starts to play. Needing an escape from my thoughts, I join in. The rules are complicated. We are collecting suits and I am collecting the wrong ones. I lose and the guy next to me clips a clothes peg on my ear. It doesn't hurt too much, just a dull grip on my lobe. I lose again and cop another peg. The first one begins to throb and I lose again. The pegs are like alligator clips. I want to rip them off but the men shake their scarred heads when my hands move close. Soon I have three pegs on each ear and the pain is incredible. I want them off. I want to go to sleep and escape this stupid game. I clench my fists so tight I bend the cards, and I lose again.

There is the narrowest slip of moon floating over the sea. I reach out and cup it in my palm, make an 'o' of my fingers and view it through that. There are wet sacks beneath me. It is cold and I have no other clothes. I slip into my boardbag and zip it around my neck. It smells like damp carpet and coconut wax and is gritty with sand. The motor hums like a bored child and I try to sleep but I am too tired.

The crew is asleep. The skipper is at the wheelhouse, drinking arak and steering a course by his stars. He offers me the bottle and I take a swig. It is harsh with a foul back-taste. There is an oily paste over my tongue and I wonder how many times that bottle has been refilled and with what.

Through the chipped screen, the sea is a tangle of scratches. The skipper pushes his stumpy finger against the plastic. '*Bintang ini*,' he says. Shrugging, I look where he is pointing. Language is a broad ocean and we are fish gupping at its surface, sipping each other's words and spitting them back. Then I remember Bintang Beer and how it has a star on its label. He is saying something about a star. '*Bintang saya!*' he jabs his thumb at his own chest. That must be his star, the one he is steering by. I squint through the dirty plastic at his tiny sun. It burns red, then blue – beautiful, in an empty black sea between the continents of star groups. Now he has shown me his star there is nothing left to say. We don't have each other's words, so we just stand dumbly looking at the ocean, waiting for his boat to get us where we are going.

It is coldest just before the sun comes up. When it does, the sea gets new – the crests of its waves shine, the troughs deepen. I watch for dolphins. A school of flying fish leap at the sky, wings like petrol rainbows. They smack against the boat, land on the deck. The crew gathers them for breakfast but I haven't the stomach for them. I hold one in my hand until its eye gets glassy and its wings begin to dry, then I drop it into the sea.

The day heats up. The steel gunnels of the boat burn my back. I crawl next to the wheelhouse but the sun is soon overhead, narrowing the shadows. My lips crack. The skipper offers me water but the bottle looks old. I remember Mum's first rule. I remember Lakey Beach.

And when I remember Lakey's of course I remember Beck. She is a dangerous thought circling my mind like a plane over a fog-bound airport.

The tips of my ears blister. The crew pulls out a tarp and

rigs it from the wheelhouse to the stern. A guy with a harelip and an old blue tattoo calls me. I sway across the splintery deck to the square of shade.

A bottle of arak and a pack of cards are placed in the middle of their circle. Mr Harelip puts his arm over my shoulder. His shirt is sleeveless and his wet forest of armpit hairs nuzzles my shoulder. I want to shrug him off but he puts the bottle of arak to my lips and I drink. I splutter, spraying arak over the cards.

Harelip laughs and says something to the crew. They laugh. I try to smile but it's not funny. I don't know what is going on.

They deal me a hand but I am too sun-drunk to play. Even when I wasn't muddled by the heat, I didn't get their game, with its clothes pegs and stupid rules. I know they cheat.

I curl up in my boardbag. The crew play cards and argue with each other. More plastic bottles appear, corked with plastic bags. I study Harelip's tattoo – a *wayang kulit* character. It takes up his whole forearm and is sliced with deep scars so that one leg and one arm are disconnected. He talks fast, smoking kretek and slapping cards on the deck.

I close my eyes and the smell of clove smoke and diesel and the metallic edge of fish blood washes over me. The noise of the card players and the engine float further and further away.

I hear Castro's voice.

∗ ∗ ∗ ∗ ∗

Castro and I are eight. I have a six-three pintail I scored for twenty bucks at a garage sale. A shitty old board – my first. Castro has a twinnie with the glass job from hell. His board is so heavy we have to carry it in shifts along the beach. It is solid blue, with big, knobby warts of wax on the deck.

We walk the shore from Torquay to Jan Juc and surf the corner. We think we're shit-hot but we stay away on the big days. Tear up the plaza on our skateboards. Eventually we take on *Bird Rock* and then make the move to *Winki*. We own that wave for a while, know every bump and flat spot in the reef.

It is Castro that reels Aldo on board. We need transport to make the break south. To get to those places Mum will never drive us to. Deep water scary spots that Castro loves. He gets so amped in the car on the way, he's bouncing like a maniac on the seat. Aldo growls at him but he keeps right on bouncing. He doesn't give a shit.

It is an obvious path west to the big juice of the Southern Ocean and then further on to Margaret River.

But Castro doesn't make it.

Further back. On hot days, Castro comes to my house and we set the sprinkler up on the lawn. Dad spreads out a sheet of black poly and we grease it with washing-up liquid. Man, do we get some speed. I nail myself on our fence one year, break a finger and Mum stops the game for good. This is the year Dad leaves . . .

We build a cubby in the jacaranda – me and Castro. We

rope packing crates in the branches and shoot the neighbour's cat with frozen peas . . .

Castro and me – our feet pulling strings of sticky tar from the playground. Footy cards and the hot smell of wattle dust. He is quick with his mouth and never gets in fights. Girls love the shit out of him for that.

There are thousands of Castro-shaped holes in my life with pinpricks of light shining through them. I can't help being drawn to his memory. He was most of what made me okay.

* * * * *

I am shocked awake by shouting. It is dark. The crew is still playing cards and drinking. There are twelve empty arak bottles littering the deck. There are seven men. One is cooking, hunched over a stove, stirring noodles with a long, curved knife. He takes the pot from the boil with his bare hands and grabs a twenty-litre kerosene container. Pulling the lid off, he flings it towards the ocean. And with the stove still burning, he slots in a funnel. I hold my breath while he refuels, and wait for the whole lot to explode in a volcano of kero flame. But he keeps it under control, eventually slopping the cooking pot back on the stove.

There is more shouting from the card circle. Harelip shoves the guy next to him and he falls over, slamming into the deck. Blood winds down his birth-marked face. With a silver flare, a knife appears. Birthmark twists the blade at Harelip so he can see its shine.

Suddenly a bright light slices across the sea like the edge of a machete. The skipper lurches out of the cabin and screams at his men. Birthmark hides his knife. The cook kills the stove. One by one the lamps are snuffed and the boat plummets into darkness. The engine is silenced. The only noise is the tocking of water on the hull.

I stare into the dark with my breath held. What are we hiding from? The light sweeps again, falling twenty metres short of our boat. It stops. Then the sharp attack of rifle fire hammers across the ocean. In the path of bright water, coins of light are spat into the air. I drop to the deck, smelling the oiled wood, and wait for my scalp to be peeled open by bullets. The rifle chatters into the empty night, the sharp noses of cartridges searching for something solid. Nearby, a man weeps. My crotch is wet.

The light sweeps on, fanning across the sea, touching nothing but the lazy rolls of swell. A motor sputters to life and I trace the searchlight and the sound to a grey shadow grazing the sea. The noise shrinks, the light dissolves. We are left in dark and silence. We wait with our jaws clamped in fear, our hearts roaring blood into our ears.

Finally, our lamps flare and the smiling faces of the crew appear like masks.

'Who was that?' I ask the cook.

But he just shakes his head and sparks up his leaking stove. The others drift back to their game of cards. Birthmark and Harelip sit opposite each other, smiling and touching the pegs on their ears.

At the wheelhouse, the skipper offers me a kretek, lights one himself and peers through the cloud of smoke at the dark sea. It must be habit for him to look hopefully out this window. I wonder what he is doing here and why the hell he agreed to take me to Pulau Badak? What is in it for him? Who is hunting him and his crew with searchlights and automatic rifles?

There are too many questions. Ones that can't be answered unless you speak the language and know the people. And even then, I don't think I could ever get to the bottom of anything in this foreign place.

I imagine this skipper stumbling into Torquay. What would he make of the surfshops, the bikini girls, the summer blow-ins, the skaters, the surfers, the fishoes? Sometimes travel can feel like being trapped on another planet.

There is a sharp cry from outside, the chang of metal on metal. The skipper tosses a loop of rope over the wheel and I follow him out. Harelip and Birthmark are at it again. This time they both have knives. The crew gives them the widest circle they can afford but, as Harelip and Birthmark lunge at each other, they stumble over crates and coils of rope. The lamps throw dull moons over the deck. Men trip, hold themselves against the steel gunnels. It is like a cockfight, the onlookers avoiding a slash from polished blades. Everyone is keen to back a winner.

The skipper barks at them. This is crazy shit, like a gunfight on a plane. They will kill us all if they don't calm down. But they don't listen. Birthmark jumps at Harelip who trips backwards, his knife gliding free in a low arc to the sea.

If this was a movie it would happen in slow motion. If it was a science fiction movie, I would halt the action, slip in, and pull the kero tin out of the way.

Harelip lands beside the tin, nudging it with his shoulder. It balances for a second on its rim, rolls gently to one side, then rocks over. Fuel glug-glugs over the deck. The cook jumps forward to rescue the tin but he kicks the stove. It flips onto the deck spilling blue flame.

A boat burning at night is a lonely thing. It is a new sun in a coal-black universe. It is the only thing alive in the whole sea apart from me. I can no longer hear the horrible cries of the skipper, just the roar of diesel and wood firing up the sky.

My fingers are burnt from swimming through the fiery sea. The heat is melting the wax on my board. There is no way I could have saved the crew.

I remember fishing with my father one night on the pier at Lorne. He told me sailors never learn to swim. If they fall into the water, they die quickly. Their boots drag them under, wet wool jumpers hold them still as their lungs fill with the sea.

But surely some of the crew will have found something to cling to – an empty fuel drum, a square of hull. But this is only hope trying to shine through my desperation and loneliness.

I am alone. I have nowhere to go.

I try to find the skipper's star. There is no moon so the sky is swarming with them. They are buzzing in clusters, in ones and twos, and in the big syrupy band of the Milky Way. I recognise the Saucepan and the Southern Cross – its pointer showing me the way south. If I paddle directly south, I will skip Australia by a thousand clicks, maybe more. As if I could paddle that far. It would be like reaching for the horizon. My only hope is another boat.

Until then, should I sit tight and save my energy? How long will I last out here with no water and the sun ready to fry me and serve me to the fish? I think of my Lonely Planet, sitting useless in some robber's hut on Lombok. It was never there for me anyway. I never fully trusted that book.

The only things I am sure of now are that the boat is gone and Pulau Badak is somewhere out in the night. If the island exists at all.

I search hard for the skipper's star. *Bintang saya*. It is now my star. He left it to me when he died in that clot of burning oil. Of all the losses I have had on this trip, this feels the biggest. Even though I hardly knew the guy. Everyone else that shot through, I could have followed. It is still possible that I could catch up with them. Maybe even Beck. But the skipper is lost to me forever. I remember the moth that entered the flame at Granny's in Bajawa. The smell of it burning.

I only hope Castro is still within reach.

My star should be floating by itself in its own dead sea.

It flashes blue and red. But there are so many stars up there. Too many.

I paddle away from the boat. My hand dipping into the blackness. I am wearing my green shorts. They are the Goddess's favourite colour. I escaped her once; will she spare me now? Will she protect me? Or will she rush up and tangle me in her long blue limbs, her wild hair? I try to swallow my fear, try not to think about what is below me. The old Sasak said the mountains were the place of the gods, and humans live in the lowlands. But the sea; the sea is seething with demons. Demons with round black eyes and filed sharp teeth.

Sharks would be rolling under me now. The boat breaking up, the frantic mashing of the water by the crew will have them excited. Their blunt snouts will be trembling. I am up here, in their sky – soft as cloud – waiting for their knife-blade teeth.

Then, I see the star. I see it! *Like a diamond in the sky*. I paddle for it, shooting my way across the sea and up into the sky, where black meets black. No stopping. No holding back.

A whip-crack wakes me. It is still dark. Another crack, like far-off gunfire but more familiar. Again. Then a rumble, like mortar fire.

I strain my eyes to see what is there but the darkness is too complete. I can almost make out a silhouette but when I concentrate, it disappears like a mirage. With nothing left to lose, I paddle towards the whip-cracks. They get louder. And louder.

Now I *know* what they are. Waves breaking over coral. The sound of tubes flattening on themselves, air blasting out across steep shoulders. I have arrived blind to a reef break. I have made land.

Almost.

In *Endless Summer*, the first one – the classic corny one that went to the breaks before they were known – where the boys scored waves in Ghana and Tahiti and sand-surfed the dunes to Cape St Francis before developers built condos on the shore and stuffed the surf forever. When they first hit the break off Dakar in Senegal, they went easy, sussing things out carefully before they cut sick. And that is what I am doing now – just getting the place wired before I catch one safe wave to shore.

I am letting the sets build and roll underneath me, tuning-in to where they are breaking, timing the lulls. I am listening for shallow spots in the reef and for the waves that will close out. The bigger ones are definitely shutting down, the smaller ones are breaking further in but it is too dangerous to wait inside.

Everyone talks about night surfing, but how many actually do it? Those who are crazy enough mostly do it *because* they are insane. I tried it once at *Margarets* but that was for Castro, and the waves were tiny, hardly there. If someone does it when it is big, then they are really stupid. If they do it at a break they have never surfed before, with big waves, then they deserve a broken back.

But I have no choice. I need to get to shore. I have thought about waiting until daybreak, but what if I get swept away by the current? Some of these islands are atolls, ringed by coral reefs. When the tide moves out, tonnes of water go with it. I will be vomited into the ocean. Or what if the swell picks up and I can't get through? Do I wait for it to die? Which would last longest – the swell or me?

I have weighed it all up and I have to go now.

This set seems good – not too huge – but with enough grunt to carry me over the coral and onto the beach. I can hear the rumble of the shorebreak and it seems reachable. I let a wave pass under me and then paddle for the next one. I am just going to lie and let the wave do the work. No fancy shit even though it's a left-hander – a goofy-footer's dream.

It starts to swell like a bloated corpse beneath me. There is no backing out. If I try to pull back I will cop a certain drilling. The wave pushes hard beneath me and I am dragged down the face. Instinctively, stupidly, I jump to my feet. Suddenly, without meaning to, I am surfing an unknown coral reef in the dark.

But it feels good. I can hear the wave behind me, shouting whitewater at my back. I shift some weight onto my front foot, get a little more speed. I am flying now. All it needs is a high spot in the reef and I am cactus.

But it doesn't happen. What does happen is a cool, smooth wall and I drag my hand in it just to know it is there. I can hear the shorebreak now. The wave starts to steepen. I pull high and over the back, landing on my belly as the wave closes-out on the beach. I turn and paddle like hell for the shore, moving quickly over the retreating foam.

The nose of my board hits the sand first. I roll off and jog up the beach. I huddle above the high tide mark, shivering in the dark beneath the rustle of coconut trees.

And now what?

12 Heart of darkness

We used to play the game, Castro and I. The one where we were shipwrecked on a desert island and we'd get to bring ten things: board, wax, rashie, beer, dim sims, *Tracks*, swimsuit model, generator, VCR, surf vids. What about electricity, Castro?

I count up what I have. I get to three and stop: board, rashie, bright-green boardies. I think about including my legrope but I reckon that it's actually part of the board.

Do I count this coconut? Inside, it is full of cool, sweet water. Outside, it is a green bank vault and I have no way to blow it open. I have bounced it off the rocks and stabbed it with sharp stones. I have lobbed it into the shorebreak and dropped it from a tree. I even tried gnawing at it with my teeth but there are only a few small brown bruises on its tough skin.

I remember the movie where Tom Hanks fell out of the sky onto a deserted island and he had the same problem. I fell asleep and woke when he was escaping – sailing his homemade boat over the reef at *Cloudbreak*. If only I was more into Tom maybe I'd have learnt how to open this thing.

And if I had ten wishes for this desert island, they would be nine litres of water and an axe to crack this frigging nut.

There is not much to do but wait. Maybe there is water further inland but if I leave the beach and the rescue party arrives I will be stuck here forever. I could go for a surf – the waves are mind-blowing – but I don't have the energy. I sit and watch wave after wave rip across the reef. I was lucky to have made it in last night; the swell has picked up. It must be at least eight to ten now, and firing like a cracker.

I try to sleep but I keep dreaming of Castro and Beck swimming away from me. I wake in a panic, gasping for air. Once there is this green-lipped lizard staring at me from the deck of my board. He darts off when I croak, 'Hello'.

I have dropped so far that I am struggling to see where I fell from. Timor is a million light years away. Can't believe I was scared then, and of what? Water? People? Maybe I was onto something though, because water and people are the things that brought me here and I am certainly deep in the shit.

But even after all the heavy stuff that has gone down, I am okay. I'm trying hard not to think about what happened to the crew of the *Perompak*. And Beck leaving was a punch in the guts. As for Niagara – I can still see him in the *becak* on Jalan Malioboro, Belacan's snout snooping over his shoulder. His leaving was hard. But at least I have no one left to lose.

Except Castro. And did I really have him at the start? Or was it all just a dream?

Maybe I haven't got what I came for. But I'll make it home somehow, with a swag of stories. That stitches some of the cuts I feel inside. Travel's not really about magic mushie T-shirts and sunburn; it's about the stories you make and the people that make them real. They're your own stories, not Lonely Planet copies. Dramas and comedies and bizarre horror movie plots. That's how every person travelling the one road can complete their own journey at the same time.

These stories have taught me something about myself. They are about people and places, and things I have done that I would never have had the guts to do at home. I feel fuller deep down, like I have grown to fit my body. Despite all the bad things that have happened, I know it's me that's pushed myself along this path and getting this far is really something. It really is. I know I can't blame anyone else for the mess I am in, but on the flipside, those honey-tasting moments are all mine.

I wonder how Niags is doing? I gave him a hard time. He was an okay guy. Helped me out more than once. Sure there was that drop-in bullshit at *Lakey*'s but it isn't his fault he's a kook. And he was the one that saved me in the end – scraped me off the reef, brought me sweet tea and bananas when

I nearly died of fever. I wonder if *he* got what he came for? Unlike me, he admitted the ghost he was trailing wasn't alive; even if he kept on trying to bring Max back with all that travel voodoo: following his road, getting a dog, surfing. It was as if he was trying to *be* Max. And then his uncle turned out to be his dad. It's hard to know if that was a bonus or the worst bloody thing in the world. He discovers Max is his father and then he's sure that the only place he's going to find him is in a box at the bottom of a deep hole in some place called Locust Grove. Finds him and loses him in the same moment. *Bad joss*, he would say.

Out at the break, it is a solid ten-foot and perfect. No sections, no close-outs, just big long walls of water. Then on top of a rising wave, I see a fin. It rises. A curved back, an echo of sunlight over it. Another fin. And another. Dolphins.

They push with the wave, shoot through it as it breaks and then rocket out the back. I lob my coconut into the shorey and walk down the beach. They are onto another one, rising and falling in formation, dancing with the water.

And then from the far right of the break, I see a figure paddling a board. I try to blink away the mirage but it stays there like the spots you get when you push on your eyelids. The surfer paddles until he is in the take-off zone. The dolphins rise around him then push towards the far point. He goes for a wave, takes a massive drop, carves a big bottom turn, arches, then stalls for the tube. The wave barrels, spitting lumps of angry water over his head. He holds out his arms but he can't touch the sides. It is that big, that perfect. The tube begins to shut. The guy speed-crouches. He is tanking-it, moving at light speed. He is almost out of the eye when it closes.

It blasts water down the line, ripping the shoulder from the wave. There is eight foot of white water screaming at the sky. I feel the sand shake. The foam spreads like an atomic cloud, mushrooming over the shining reef. I look for the dark shape of the surfer but there is nothing. Nothing.

Then he pops up and paddles wide, escaping the next wave, which has already started to rip across the reef. I can't believe he is going out for another shot. That was way too heavy. This is so Castro. His style, his full-on commitment. I want to call out but there is no way he will hear me.

He lumbers into another huge tube. Bigger than the last. This time he makes it, rockets out of the barrel and leaps over the shoulder – crazy birdman, twigged black against the sky.

I watch him get ten waves like that. Then the tide changes and the swell drops and he paddles in. I jump to my feet and run to meet him. It's Castro. I am so happy I want to shout. This whole trip has been worth it. I found what I was looking for. I never gave up hope.

I reach him just as he is leaving the shorebreak. His long hair is pressed flat to his skull. It is grey. The guy is ancient. Too old to be surfing like that. Too old to be Castro.

'You scored some pearlers out there,' I say, trying to keep

the flatness out of my voice. I have to remember that I am shipwrecked and this is another human being.

He just looks at me with his sun-wrecked eyes. Salt water streams from his nose.

I offer him my hand. 'Goog's the name.'

'I know who you are,' he says, taking it slowly. 'Call me Max.' He pauses for a while to let his words catch up with my racing mind. 'Walk with me. I have someone who is looking forward to seeing you.'

We climb the rhino's horn – a sharp spire of volcanic rock that rises at the far end of Pulau Badak. A path twists around the horn, chiselled deep into the rock and jungle. There is a vertical fall of forty metres from here onto the canopy of trees below. I am following Max who is jogging up the steep track, his board tucked underneath his arm.

'Marlow sailed in to the heart of darkness looking for Kurtz,' says Max over his shoulder.

'What are you talking about?' My head is buzzing and I am struggling for breath.

'Don't tell me you haven't read Conrad.'

'The quote on the back of the map?'

Max stops and turns. 'One and the same. In *Heart of Darkness*, Conrad sent Marlow into the Congo to search for a madman called Kurtz. Have you seen the movie *Apocalypse Now*?'

'Yeah,' I say, vaguely remembering some movie set in

Vietnam. Dad had got all excited about it. There was a scene where a crazy colonel sends a guy out surfing while bombs are blasting water into the air and the beach is burning with napalm. The waves were crap.

'That movie is the same story as *Heart of Darkness*. And that story is the same as yours.'

This guy is crazy. I should return to the beach and chat to my coconut.

'You are Marlow.' He points to the sea. 'That ocean is the river Marlow travelled to get to Kurtz.' He points to the top of the hill. 'Up there is your Heart of Darkness.' Then he smiles. 'But you'll get through it, Gurg. And you'll reach the truth. The truth is like a speck of light wrapped in a bundle of dark.'

I have no idea what Max is talking about. He must be doing some serious drugs.

'Where's Niagara?' he asks.

'He's gone home.'

'Jasper promised.' Max smacks his hand on his board. 'He promised!'

'Jasper?'

'Never mind,' says Max, picking up his board and starting up the track again.

'Wait!' I shout after him. 'What do you know about Jasper? What's going on?'

I don't catch him until we are almost at the top of the horn. The ground levels out and the trees thin until we enter a clearing. It is littered with about thirty boulders the size of small caravans and against each of these is a lean-to of branches and palm fronds.

Max holds out his arms. 'This is it – your Heart of Darkness.'

Eyes appear at the entrances to the shelters. Arms with tattoos, faces striped black with charcoal. Men step out. They are wearing jungle fatigues and carrying automatic rifles. One of them has a harelip and another, the greasy forearms of the *Perompak's* mechanic. A third is the boat's cook.

'You . . .' I move towards them. 'Where . . .'

I feel Max's strong hand gripping my elbow. 'This way, Gurg. He'll explain.'

He leads me deep into the settlement and up to a huge boulder in the centre. There is a strangler fig flexing its narrow fingers into the stone, rupturing its heart with thick roots. Max points to a three foot wide crack in the boulder. 'He's in there.'

'Who?' I ask, but the surf-poet just turns and jogs back the way he came.

I lean my board against the rock and take a deep breath. There are eighty or a hundred eyes staring at me. It is silent apart from the chirr of insects.

I run my hand over the rock and into the crack. It is darker than a *wayang* night in there. From the camp, eyes are drilling into my shoulders, stirring the fine hairs on my neck. Pushing my foot into the shadows, I step inside. It is cool and dark, but as I move further into the rocky corridor I see the glow from kero lamps. The corridor opens into a cave. Bats creak against each other on the roof, cockroaches rattle down the walls.

There is a carved desk – shot through with wormholes – in the centre of the cave, with a pile of papers stacked loosely in the middle. Beside the papers is a handgun. There is also a pouch of rolling tobacco and a roll of extra strong mints. The Tubes card, the one with Castro's message, is propped against the gun barrel. I haven't seen this card since the night bus to Yogya. How the hell it got here is too much to think about. I slip it into my pocket. Proof.

'Hey, mate.'

I recognise the voice but it shocks me. It shunts in from the past like a train, hitting me hard with steel and steam. I turn round and I see him. He is standing like he used to, one hip higher than the other, showing me his throat. I think of picking up the handgun and blowing him away.

He says, 'You wouldn't shoot your old man, would you, Nipper?'

I remember Granny's prediction – that I would find who I was not looking for. I don't know what to say. It has been too many years and this is too strange a time and place for a reunion.

All I can come up with is, 'I'm nineteen, Dad, I'm not your Nipper anymore.'

'You'll always be my Nipper, mate.'

He ruffles my hair and his big hand smells of tobacco and kerosene. I used to dream about him when I was younger, but he grew faint in my memory like some underexposed negative. I couldn't even picture his face after my twelfth birthday. Mum binned all the photos. Cut him out of the albums so that every shot looked like some cracked half of a jigsaw piece.

I am not looking up at him anymore, not like when I was ten. Now he looks small and old and a bit crooked in the back. There are white crow's feet arrowed at the sea-blue of his eyes. His hair has the first snow of winter nuzzled at his temples. If I wanted, I could wrestle him to the ground and make him taste the damp, batshit earth.

'Cat gotcher tongue, Nipper?'

No, Dad, nine years of silence have got my tongue. Nine years of staring at your one postcard and waiting for a call that never came – that's pretty much got my tongue too.

'We gotta bit of catchin up to do, Nipper.'

'Look, I don't want you to call me Nipper.'

Dad looks like I just boxed him hard in the head. 'Why?'

'I'm too old now. The time for calling me Nipper is over. If you'd hung around and watched me grow up you'd know that.'

Dad grabs the pouch of rolling tobacco from the desk. He rolls a cigarette one-handed like he used to, big fingers working the paper like a surgeon. The rollie comes out thin and perfect – a greyhound, he used to call it. He pushes it all the way in his mouth and wets it down, smoothing it in one action then reaching for his matches. There is the heavy blast of sulphur and then a cloud of smoke as he exhales his first drag. The lines around his eyes relax.

'So whadda I call yer then?' he says, picking a strand of tobacco from his tongue.

'Well my mates call me Goog.'

'Then Goog it is.'

'But Greg will do.'

He sucks a little air through his teeth. 'Tough customer, eh? Fancy sparring with yer old man?' He slips his smoke into the corner of his mouth and bounces on his toes with his big fists protecting his face.

I shake my head at him. 'I'd punch the living shit out of you.'

'Yer reckon, do yer?' He darts out a quick left at my head and I dodge it.

'I don't want to spar with you.'

'Sure you do, Nipper. Like we used to. Down on the sand. When you were only a foot-and-a-fart high.'

He shoots a right at me and I stumble over the table. I don't remember us ever sparring.

'I don't want to fight you, Dad.'

'Who said anything about fightin? This is sparrin. Different animal altogether.'

'I just want to go home.'

'No you don't, Nipper. Don't you wanna know why I had you brought here?'

He still has his fists up protecting his face. Smoke shuts one eye. He looks like a flyweight.

'If *you* brought me here then I do want to know. I want to know everything.'

'Well it wasn't xackly my idea. More Jasper.'

'Jasper?'

'Yep, yer old mate from the Nullarbor.'

'He's no mate of mine.'

'Aw, look, he's awright.'

'He's a bloody psycho!'

'There is a bit of that about the man, but he means well.'

'He's not a bloody Great Aunt or anything, Dad. His best mates are Neo-Nazis. The guy had something to do with Castro disappearing. He just about destroyed our mate Aldo.'

'By the sounds of it, your mate Aldo was no saint either. He was a Neo-Nazi himself. Got what he deserved. Besides, alls I ever wanted was you here with me.'

He opens his palm and slaps me on the chest. 'So, come on, Nipper. Give it a shot. I'll give yer first punch free.'

I ignore his chin stuck out for me to whack, his two fingers tapping it. 'Why'd you bring me here?' I ask.

Dad stops tapping his chin. 'Me and Maxy wanted our boys. Things are hottin up round here and we needed to see youse. The army's been sniffin round like flies on shit. They's bin doin raids, strikes on our camps in Sumatra. It's not goin to last much longer. Somethin bad's about to go down. I needed to see you and splain a few things.' He throws his half-smoked cigarette on the dirt floor and grinds it in with his foot.

'What do you want to explain?'

'I dunno, just things. Time comes when a dad's gotta talk to his son, man-to-man.'

'What are you on about? I'm a bit old for the facts of life.'

'Naw, Nipper. Portant stuff. Gotta splain things that have been buzzin through my head like a swarm of bloody bees. Why I left youse and all that.'

I wait for him to start. It's a big stretch of water that separates us and he's going to have to nail his raft together before I'll make my move.

He rubs his hair with both his hands like he is shampooing it. 'Kids is tricky, see. You have em one day and the next they're grown and they want to know everything, even things you can't hardly splain.' He begins to roll another smoke. 'You was always a smart little tacker.' Shaking his head, he chuckles at the memory. 'Always pullin shit apart. Couldn't put it back together to save yersel, but we'd find watches and clocks and radios with their guts all spilled out on the kitchen table. I'd shout at you for it, but it never stopped you. You were too curious, see. Wanted to know how things were inside.' Pushing the smoke in his mouth, he puts a match to it. 'Not me, I'm not like that. You got that from your mother. Me, I'm happy if things are as they are. But you was always naggin at me. "Tell me about the war, Daddy. What was it like? Were you a big hero, Daddy?" And Priya's comin up behind you and she's startin to act like you, and it's gettin too much, see. And Mum's sayin, "They're only kids, Bill. Leave them be."

And it's all gettin too crowded and hard and then I meet this bloke and he says he's goin out West and there's a bit of coin to be made in the mines and he's gotta spare seat . . .' He drifts off until his words are hanging with the bats from the roof of his cave.

'And it was that easy?' I ask him.

'It wasn't easy, Nipper. It was never easy. I bin carrying this with me for nine bloody years. It's been like the cancer just eatin me out from the inside. I had to know what was happening with you and Mum and Priya. I had to.'

'Well, we're just fine. I mean you stuffed up our lives and broke everything that was important but we're just doing brilliant.'

'Don't be like that, Nipper.'

'If you call me Nipper one more time, I'll . . .'

'Punch me, Nipper? You gonna punch me?' Dad is up on his toes again, bouncing like a butterfly and stinging like a bee. He catches me one in the chest and it knocks the wind from me. I feel the buzz of adrenalin in my thighs.

'Leave it, Dad.'

'Come on, Nipper. For old time's sake.' He jabs a right at me and, as I dodge it, it gets me hard in the shoulder, throwing me off balance and onto the dirt. He laughs at me.

And then things go dark and I jump up and smack him hard in the face and, as he falls, I am on him, belting him again and again. And I am crying and there is blood and salt-tears on both of us and he is still laughing and he doesn't know how much I needed him all these years and how much he has taken away with this one meeting. And I hate him, so I hit him again and again.

And then I feel hands tight around my arms and I am flying backwards and I am shouting and crying and spitting at my dad who is curled up in the dirt. I feel the cold weight of steel on my neck and it sobers me. I slump forward and wait for a bullet.

'Leave him,' says Dad through a handful of blood.

And they drop me on the ground and I get up and look at Dad, broken in the dirt; and, as our eyes lock for that three seconds, I see something trying to break free. He reaches out his hand but I turn and run down the dark corridor and out into the light. The eyes are still there, burning even under the harsh sun.

'What are you looking at?' I scream. 'Have you never seen a ghost before?'

I *am* a ghost; walking in a dream – a *wayang* dream. I am a shadow puppet, holes of light burning through me, jerking on bamboo sticks.

I pick up my board and run towards the path. The Eyes grab guns. The Eyes grab machetes. They wait for orders that never come. I am so fast down that path that I slide the two k's to the beach.

'Gurg, you just don't know what it has been like for your old man.'

Max and I are sitting watching the break from the beach. He has an old copy of *Heart of Darkness* in his lap. The cover is salt-stained and riddled with tiny holes. There is power in this book, he is sure of it.

I am trying to figure out a way off this island. Maybe even paddling out on my board. Taking on the break in reverse, this time in daylight. Even with my green shorts.

'Being a father is no simple thing,' says Max.

'How would you know? You didn't even admit to being Niagara's father.'

Max nods. He opens his book at random. There are black clouds of mould obscuring words; entire paragraphs shut down by mildew. 'I can't read this anymore,' he says. 'The words have gone. This place steals everything eventually. Soon, even my memories will be eaten through by this wet, salt air.'

For once I see through what he is saying. 'You want to know about Niagara.'

Max swallows softly and looks out at the white fringe peeling across the reef.

'And I need to know about Dad.'

'You're right, Gurg, I do need to know about Niagara but as for your dad – I think it would be best if you asked him.'

'He won't tell me anything now.'

'How do you know if you don't ask him.'

'Look, have we got a deal here? Niagara for Dad. One for one.'

Max looks at me hard, but I hold the stare.

'Deal,' he says eventually, offering me his hand. 'What you want to know?'

'I want to know everything. Who he is? Why he had Jasper bring me here? The whole package.'

Max's eyebrows shoot up his forehead and I am suddenly reminded of Niagara. 'You can't know everything, Goog. That much knowledge would kill you,' he says. 'I tell you as much as I know.' He shuts the book and places it face down in the sand.

'The first, and most important, thing you should know is that your dad is a great man. He does everything for these people, for the struggle in the north.'

'But he's done shit-all for me for nine years.'

'And he wants to make that better.'

'You can't just *make* that better. You can't just suck back nine years and make it good by calling a guy you barely know "Nipper"; putting your arm round his shoulder and trying to be his mate. It doesn't work like that, Max.'

'See that break?' says Max, shifting gear.

'Yeah, I see it! I didn't bloody see it the first time, though. Nearly killed myself coming over it in the dark. Bet dear old Dad was behind that one too.'

'I watched that break for two years before even going out,' says Max, ignoring me. 'Saw it in all kinds of weather, all tides. I know that reef better than I know the back of my hand.' He shows me his hand – white moons on his nails, mosquito scars, knuckles like reef knots. 'When you know something that well you kind of hope it will forgive you your little mistakes. Like today. I blew it in that tube, badly, but luckily the break decided not to finish me.'

We stare at the break for a minute and then Max continues, 'Your Dad invested ten good years in you. It wasn't easy, not with what he had to live with. Not with what happened to him in Nam.'

'And what *did* happen in Vietnam, Max? He told me jack shit about the war.'

Max picks up a handful of sand, flings it at the beach. 'You should ask him that.'

'He won't tell me. I know he won't.'

I can see Max is thinking as he pours sand between his hands. 'We all met over there, you know. Your dad, Jasper and me. In Vung Tau, some crapass bar we drank at when we got time off from the fighting. Said if we made it through we'd find each other again. We were family over there. You see so many get blown up, shot to ribbons. It's bad, Gurg. It's worse than bad; ten steps worse. But the friendships you make – those ones are for keeps.' He carries on pouring sand as he talks, never taking his eyes off the grains falling in their thousands to the beach.

'Jasper had the best chance of making it, of course. He loved everything about the place, a born scammer. Selling narcotics to the troops, buying antiques. But your dad, he was scared the whole time. He was way too gentle for that war.

They made him clear out the tunnels. The Cong dug tunnels, see, miles of them, rigged with trip wires and booby traps. Pits jammed with sharpened stakes. Your dad never wanted to go in and clear them, but orders are orders.

'One day he came across one with a Vietcong jammed up a blind alley. He was supposed to go back in there and get him out.' Max's eyebrows drop at the corners like he is remembering something bad. 'You can't take a gun in the tunnels, see, no room . . .' He drifts off, dumps his fist into the sand. 'We had to get him out of Nam. Jasper smuggled him through Cambodia and Thailand. He got him home. But he was all wrecked inside, blamed himself for every black bag he saw on the evening news. We all lost something over there. I think your dad lost more than most.

'He drifted around for a while and then he met your mom. I'd hear from him every now and then – when he got married, when he had you and your sister. And then things started to go wrong and I got word from Kalgoorlie that he had left and was working there. That he was drinking too much and getting in trouble. I was here setting up by then. So, I got Jasper to go and fetch him.'

'What's the deal with Jasper?'

Max laughs. 'Who knows? The man wears a big cloak. No one knows who he really is but if you need something done, then he's the one. He's a coyote, see, a people-smuggler. And he's a master forger as well – he can duplicate handwriting, make passports out of paper and card, even prints up his own money. Multi-skilled, I think they call it now. Ink instead of blood. Borders mean nothing to him – they are porous – he just turns people into smoke and blows them through.'

Max gets up and brushes the sand from his shorts. 'Let's take a walk,' he says. 'I need to put some queries your way.'

He has forgotten his copy of *Heart of Darkness* so I pick it up.

We cross the point between two bays. Our hands brush over prone shrubs and our feet pick the gentlest path between jagged rock and coral. We don't speak; it allows time for the sharp spines of truth to settle in the soft folds of my brain. My dad, Jasper and Max – three points of a triangle that has been in place since before I was born. I cannot believe I have come so far for this. This clue is the foundation stone holding up a house of cards that has been building around me since the day Castro, Aldo and I left Torquay. I can feel the pressure of too much information hammering at my temples. With my fingers, I push against the thin skin, feeling the throb of blood and the explosion of thoughts inside. I shake my head to rattle them free, feel them dislodge like shards of bone. I watch Max's chapped heels rising and falling. The long growl of surf, the secret of wind through palms. Max's feet rise and fall.

Eventually, we arrive at another beach with sand so white it looks like snow. My eyes hurt just looking at it.

'What happened to my nephew?' asks Max.

I stop and grab his arm. He looks right into my eyes as

I speak. 'He found that letter in your diary. The one from Rosa to you. From his mum.'

'What diary?'

'He had your journal. He was following your trail through the islands.'

'How did he get tha—' Max stops short, his eyes widen. 'Jasper! He said he'd fix it, not to worry. That he'd get you and Niagara here. Niagara wasn't meant to find out, not like that. Jasper always has to go one step too far. He's always bragging that he's the puppet master, that he's in control. The jackass!'

'Jasper's no jackass,' I say. 'He gets things done but he doesn't mind creating a few waves along the way. Niagara thought you were dead.'

Max buries his face in his hands. 'Oh, man.'

Another piece slips into place. 'The guy who came to see Niagara at the grocery store. The one with the accent who told him you had died. That was Jasper!'

'How many times can you abandon one boy?' Max is squeezing his scalp with his fingers. 'I left him with that power tripper, Archie.' He looks up at me. 'He made Niagara call him Sir, you know?'

I nod.

'I didn't mean it to turn out this way, Gurg. I swear.'

'So why did you leave?' I ask him. The similarities between him and my old man are too scary.

Max flinches. 'That's between me and Niagara,' he says.

I hand him his worm-riddled book. 'Well, you'd better catch up with him. He was headed to Jakarta and then home.'

'It's too late now.'

'He'll still be there. He needs to get a new passport and a ticket. It'll take him a week, easy.'

'No, it's too late for us. Too much time gone.'

'It's not too late. You should find him and explain. He deserves it.'

'What's he like?' asks Max.

'He's cool. Everyone likes him.'

'And you're sure it's not too late?' he asks.

'I'm sure.'

'Well by the same reasoning, it's not too late to give *your* father another chance.'

So I give him a chance. At night, with the rocks lit by campfires and kero lamps, we sit out the front of his cave and we talk. He has nine years to make up and I will make him work for every minute of it.

'So Maxy's off after Niagara,' he says as he hands me a cold Bintang.

'Yep,' I say, taking a sip of my beer. 'You guys have a lot in common.'

Dad smiles. 'We do, Nip—, uh, Greg. Known each other a pile of years.'

'Seems like you both know how to leave your families.'

'Look, mate. That was no easy choice. Can we just bury it and move on?'

He takes a hard slug of his beer. I can hear him swallow it above the fire, the surf, the rush of air through the jungle. We sit there in silence, then he speaks again.

'I'm glad you're here, y'know. Pleased as punch,' says Dad and squeezes my shoulder in that matey way.

I ice up my voice with cold beer and reply, 'And I am just stoked to be here.'

Dad pinches his top lip. He rolls a smoke, slowly.

'Of course,' I continue, 'it would have been better if my mate, Castro, could have been here too. But I am sure you don't really give a shit about that.'

'How is old Castro, anyway?' he asks, trying to make light conversation.

'Dead, as far as I know, thanks, Dad.'

'Shit, I'm sorry to hear that. Death is a terrible thing, but who knows if it's the end.' Dad takes a long swig of beer and stares hard into the fire. 'How's your surfin coming on?'

'Yeah, great. Been doing a bit of night-surfing lately. Some long paddles from burning boats. I suppose you had a hand in that?'

'Like I told you before, Jasper handles the details.'

'You're just shifting the blame.'

'Maybe. Most of the guys from the *Perompak* survived, y'know. They paddled broken bits of boat in on the lee side of the island. No swell there y'see. If you'd used your noggin you'd've come the same way.'

'Guess I had other things on my mind.' I grit my teeth at the memory – how hot the ocean can get before it turns to steam, what fire looks like as it rips across an oily sea.

Dad looks at the ground. Tucks his rollie behind his ear.

'Really wanted you to see all this,' he says, pointing his bottle at the fires and the khaki-covered shoulders. 'You might think it seems like a high price to pay, but I just wanted you to see it.'

'Wow, Dad. Next time just send me a frigging photo!'

'Don't be pissed off at me for wantin to see you.'

'Dad, I'm not pissed off about that. But I am pissed off at you leaving when I was ten and then sending your pet Nazi, Jasper, to stuff up my life.'

'Yeah, well what Jasper does is beyond my control.'

'Stop trying to wriggle out of it.' I sip my beer and look past the camp at the fringe of forest. 'So what is it you do here?' I ask.

'We're in the supply game. We get gear to the freedom fighters.'

'What do you supply? Food?'

'Yup.'

'Drink?'

'Yup.'

'Guns?'

'Them too.'

'So you're a gun-runner. Wow, I am so proud of you! My old man the gun-runner.'

'Easy, Nipper. It's hard for you to understan.'

'I thought you were against war.'

'I am.' He is getting agitated. He jumps up and throws a stick at the fire, sending a shower of sparks into the air. 'You haven't seen what I've seen. Villages burnin. People with so many holes they look like one of them *wayang* puppets. You're only a boy.'

'I'm nineteen, Dad. I was a boy nine years ago when you left.'

Dad shakes his head, kicks a log further into the fire. 'I was nineteen too, once. Long time ago.' He shakes his head. 'They packed me off to fight a bloody war I knew nothin about. That kinda drilled the boy outta me.

'I hated bein over there. The dreams. Shittin myself every single day, spectin a bullet in the head when we went out on a reccy. But war is a bit like bein on the drugs and once you've had a taste, you keep wandrin back, wantin it despite it bein the worst damn thing for you.

'Mates were everythin over there. There was nothing they wouldn't do fer you. Jasper came and got me when I was in a bad way, said I was needed in Indo. That long streak of duckshit saved me; gave me a reason to live again. See, this is my reason. I care about what happens to these people. They're like my family.' He tries to swallow the last bit, but it hangs in the night air like a lure.

'If you'd cared about your *family* things would have been better for us.'

'I know, mate. Don't you think I know that? But I'm talkin thousands of lives here.'

'You are a stinking bloody hypocrite!'

'I'm still your father.'

'That's a pile of shit. You gave up that right nine years ago.'

We are both on our feet with the red of the fire on our faces. We are nose to nose. I can smell tobacco and mints on his breath.

Then there is a deep roar and the sky goes orange. People are running everywhere. Dogs are howling. Another roar. Trees are burning. Entire trees going up like candles, flaring into the blue-black sky. There's a thok-thok sound and the grass around us dances and is pressed flat. Dad calls to me, but I can't hear what he is saying over the thokking and the clattering air and the chatter of guns and the roar of flames. A loudspeaker blares Indonesian and everyone is bathed in light. People run for the trees and rocks but everything is on fire. They arc onto the ground, heads lolling, legs at strange angles. Dad grabs me and runs with me to his cave.

'Raid!' he shouts as he shoves me inside.

It is pitch black; the lamps are all out. We feel our way over the walls. Dad has his hand in mine and I feel like I am ten again and he is walking with me down to the sea. Everything will be okay. He will protect me.

We move further and further into the cave and the noise

is dulled by the weight of the rock behind us. I feel the floor sloping down.

'Where are we going?' I ask but Dad is silent. His hand is the only way I know he is still there.

I can hear the knocking of water against stone and smell salt in the air. We slip into the warm ocean and I swim holding onto Dad's ankle until there is an orange glow ahead. The mouth of a sea cave frames the silhouette of a boat. Outside the forest is ablaze and the black shapes of helicopters are stabbing spears of light into the island.

Dad and I clamber over the gunnels of the boat. I sit in the stern as Dad rows us slowly out to sea.

'Where are we going?' I ask again.

He looks at me with the jungle-fire flaring over his face and says, 'I'm getting you home, Nipper.'

13 The puppet master

He is the snake, the dark dragon of my dreams. But he's still only a man. I have to remember that.

It has been over a year now since I met him and in that year he has grown in my mind like a dangerous virus. I am sick with the thought of this meeting and trying hard to battle my growling stomach. It is late afternoon, still warm, but I am shivering in the bow of the boat. I can't believe he is the only one that can help me.

Dad and I are headed up a twisted river, past mangroves and the sly bodies of crocodiles. Tall-legged herons dart slender beaks into the black waters. The air smells of wood smoke.

We made it to shore this morning, pulling into a sheltered river mouth and uncovering a fifteen foot boat with a petrol motor. Without speaking, we began motoring upriver.

Dad smiles at me. 'This is where we bring the supplies in. Mostly at night. The locals are afraid of the joint. The army too. Bad ghosts, see. Old women that live in trees, their hands and feet turned round. They reckon they eat the hearts of young blokes like you.'

As if that would scare me. What we are headed for is worse than any heart-eating old hag.

We turn into a side river – a narrow channel bearded with creepers and thick Tarzan vines. It gets narrower and narrower and we have to stop and drag the boat over dry rock. We slip back into the water and continue on without speaking.

I hear whispers in the forest. Eyes turn into white fruit hanging in clusters from vines. Trees have gaping mouths and long grey beards. Monkeys run to the ends of branches and sit, staring at us, swaying over the water and chattering to each other.

The forest gets thick with heat and it rains. The air fills with water. Drops as big as fists punch into the river and fill the hull of the boat. I bale with my hands, scared that we will sink before we get to wherever it is we are going. Dad wipes water from his eyes and squints into the white sheet ahead. These clouds are serious about trying to drown us.

We are falling into the heart of nothing. Whatever Dad is steering by keeps him motoring up river. The prow of the boat spears into the unknown.

And then the rain stops. Like a switch has been flicked. Like a tap has been shut off. The air goes still. The rain turns to steam. The river becomes smoke. We are gliding through it like ghosts.

The only sound comes from our buzzing motor. Dad's eye is swollen from our fight and his hairless arms are covered with mosquito bites. There is a *wayang* tattoo on his right bicep.

'Dad,' I whisper, climbing to the stern. He is staring into the mist, one hand on the outboard, the other dragging a wake in the river.

'Dad,' I say again. We are breathing the river mist. I suddenly have the horrible feeling it is poisonous; loaded with some drug that will pull us too far into this place and I will never find the way home.

Finally he looks at me, eyes wild for a moment, and then, slowly focussing. He smiles. 'What?'

I point at his arm. 'What's with the tatt?'

Dad takes a deep breath. The silhouette of the puppet is blurry with age, sliced through the belly with a deep scar. I think back to the night in the village near Yogya – the endless waves of music building and building, the other-world chatter of the *dalang*, the fluttering of puppets against the white screen.

'The tatts were Maxy's idea,' says Dad. 'He used to be a puppet master, a *dalang*, they call em.'

I nod, Niagara told me this already.

'When we started up, we figured we needed to remember why we was doing it. Sometimes, over years, you lose track of why. Max said tattoos would help us remember.'

'How?'

'Our people have bin puppets for so long they've forgot how to help theirselves. We're just givin them a hand to get rid of the guys pullin the sticks, as it were.'

'Haven't you just jumped in as the puppet masters?'

'No, Nipper. That's the point of the tatts,' he says, taking his hand off the outboard and turning his huge palms to the low sky. The boat coasts upstream without him. 'For us to remember that Max and me and Jasper are only here to help them be their own masters. To give it a go theirselves.'

'But the tattoos are just a symbol of them being puppets?'

'Yeah . . . and no. They're a reminder of what they were and of what they *can* be. It's them that's going to be controlling the puppet sticks in the future. They'll be the *dalangs*. Their own *dalangs*.'

Dad wipes the rain from the tattoo and continues. 'The puppets have another meaning too, Nipper. See, they're part light and part shadow. Like all of us, they got good and bad in em. It is too easy to write people off as being all good or all bad. We can all change.'

'What about you, Dad, can you change?' Maybe there is a chance. Maybe he's ready to be the dad I have always needed him to be.

Dad laughs. 'I have done a lot of changing, Nipper. I'm about all changed-out.'

I look away from him at the blacksnake river, at the faces that are sneering up at me from tree snags and hidden rocks.

The jetty has hardwood posts topped with carved masks – demon dogs, their lips pulled back to show inch-long teeth and fat rolls of tongue.

Dad says, 'We're here.' He points to a path hacked into the heavy jungle. 'You go on, I'll wait here for you.'

'No, I think you should come with me. He's your mate after all.'

'You'll be okay, Nipper.'

I crawl out on a thin limb. 'I'd feel a bit easier if you were there too.'

'Can't always be there for you. Them days are over.'

I just about say that he was never there, but it isn't true. There was a time when he was there. But now I have to go it alone. It doesn't mean I can't carry the memory of that time with me just as long as I don't let it get so heavy that it threatens the present.

I turn from Dad and the boat and start down the path. He calls out behind me. 'Look after yourself, son.'

'I'll be back soon,' I say over my shoulder.

The path curves and then drops into a gully. I cross a rope bridge strung over a small stream. Hearing a shrill whistle behind me, I turn, expecting to see my old man walking down the path on his bow legs. Instead, there is a group of four wild-looking men. Their hair is long and matted, skin black with fire soot, eyes rimmed with white clay.

The Lonely Planet would tell me to stand perfectly still, or lie on my belly and play dead. Instead, I run. I go like there is a rocket up my arse. Through spider webs as big as fishing nets and over greasy logs. Through ditches carpeted with the snaking bodies of leeches. My face is scratched, my shorts rip. I don't turn to see what is behind me and, because of this, it becomes bigger and makes me run faster.

But sooner or later I have to stop. The air is so humid it is like swallowing sump oil and I can't get enough of what I need from it. Seeing a hollow tree, I force myself inside. I listen until the barefoot thomp of the men passes by. I breathe slowly through my nose, rich damp air from the heart of this tree. I wait. I watch drops of rain falling from leaves. I count to a thousand.

Then I step into the jungle. Turning my head on one side like a dog, I listen. Nothing. No monkeys or birds, just the fat clopping of rain on leaves. That spooks me more than anything – the bare silence.

What the hell is Dad playing at? He should have come with me, or at least given some kind of warning. Why is he such a loser?

There is no real path here, just a tangle of thin scars through the forest like a network of wires. I pick one up and follow it. It forks and I take the right. It happens again and I take the left. Then a right. It is a stupid system but I have no idea of where I am going and what I am looking for. I should return to the river, the boat, my deadbeat old man, and get the hell out of here. But even if I knew where the river was, I know it is not the path I am looking for – the one that leads home.

Eventually, through the blur of green, I see a house. It is built high over the sloppy jungle floor like a boat. Its roof is a long prow, tipped at each end with a snarling dog. A huge tree looms above. Snake-like vines reach down and throttle the balcony posts. *Wayang kulit* puppets are carved into the trelliswork around the verandah. A dozen paths lead from jungle to clearing, arteries flowing into this tangled heart.

The wild men from the forest are leaning against the posts. On the upper floor – half cut by shadow – stands Jasper.

On the table are four objects: two photos of Castro; my camera – the one I pawned for a plane ticket in Margaret River; an Australian passport stuffed with rupiah. Flipping open the passport, I see it has my photo and my name.

'Your choice, my young friend,' says Jasper, his voice dripping with river slime.

My hand hovers over the objects. I decided last year that I didn't need the camera anymore. I chose real life instead of what I could see through the viewfinder. It is only a temptation because it is so familiar. Maybe one day I'll return to it. But not today.

The photos of Castro are harder. I pick one of them up.

I took this photo of him when we were at Johanna. He is handstanding in front of the camp fire. Aldo's big ugly head is in the background and the two fishoes we met that day are there too. Jasper must have flogged the roll of film when we were in WA.

I turn the photo the other way, so Castro is the right way up and the others are standing on their heads. Castro always did have a strange way of looking at everything – upside-down from everyone else. Maybe if I hadn't spent so much time staring at him from behind my lens I wouldn't have lost sight of him.

In the other photo, Castro is suntanned. The rail of his board curves into the frame. He has had long hair since primary school so it comes as a shock to see his hair short-cropped. His goatee is gone too. The air around him is washed with light.

'That photo comes with extras,' says Jasper.

'Extras?'

'Yes, my friend, extras. Information. Things you may want to know.'

'Forget it, Jasper. You're just playing with my head.' I make a move for the passport but Jasper's long-fingered hand comes down on mine.

'I'll give you one for free,' he says.

I have nothing to lose. 'Okay,' I say.

'But there are some . . . shall we say . . . conditions.'

I grit my teeth. Conditions my arse. Nothing is ever simple with Jasper. I learnt that about him last year.

He continues, 'You can't ask me directly about Castro. I won't answer anything about your dad and I will only give a "yes" or "no" answer.'

I think for a moment of the most important question, the

one that will tell me almost everything. I fish the Tubes card from my pocket, the one I stole from Dad's cave in Pulau Badak. The one I found on the summit of Gunung Rinjani.

I take it slowly, thinking about how to word this question so I don't slip up and give Jasper the chance to dodge. 'Did you, or anyone working for you, plant this card on Gunung Rinjani?'

He picks up the card, looks at it and hands it back to me. I shiver as his fingertips brush mine. Closing his eyes, he thinks for a moment. He puts his long fingers to his temples as if he is channelling a spirit.

He says, 'The answer is . . . no.'

'You didn't put it there?'

'No.'

'No one you knew put it there?'

'No.'

'How did it get there?'

'Sorry, young Goog, only one freebie.'

But I know the answer and it gives me a fresh rush of hope, hot and salty inside me. Now I have to have the photo and the extras. The passport means nothing.

But the passport means home. It means getting away from this place and back to people who know me. I could never travel forever like Beck. Because getting home makes it all complete.

'Where is my dad?' I ask Jasper.

'That question I will allow on a technicality. Your dad had

to return to Pulau Badak on urgent business; he's a father to those men the army tried to annihilate. He said he loves you and wishes you well. Says he'll write.'

Somehow it doesn't surprise me. I never expected a happy ending with dear old Dad. I can't blame him. He's just stumbling through life the best way he knows. Part light and part shadow.

The passport and the photos have equal weight. Putting my hands on both of them, I look at Jasper. He has a snaky smile, his eyes deep caves in the kero lamp gloom. Maybe everything is his fault and was from the beginning. Maybe even before I met him he was messing with my life. When did all his trickery to get me to my dad begin? When we left Torquay? In Lorne? Was Castro part of it? Was he willing or just a piece of bait Jasper used and threw away? I should try to kill this man because he is the root of everything that has gone wrong. But he holds everything that I want.

There is one other thing I should ask.

'What happened to Aldo?'

'Oh, Goog, you want it all, don't you? I *have* been interfering with your life, I admit. Maybe that is payback for what you did to me in Australia. Stealing that disk in Adelaide could have got me in a lot of trouble with Aldo's Neo-Nazi compadres. But Aldo was nothing; just a pawn in the big game. What you really want to know is how far I went with Castro? Is he alive? Did I orchestrate his disappearance? His *supposed* trip to Indonesia?'

'And did you send those eleven postcards?'

Eleven postcards? I think I have hit the mark – a lightning bolt of surprise flashes over his face, but disappears before I can be sure. Maybe Jasper only sent one – the first one.

'You'll never know if you don't take the extras package. You could have a very comfortable life here in Indonesia. I am sure your dad would be thrilled at the prospect.'

I shake my head but *I* am not sure. *I* am sick of Jasper's games. My hands are still on the passport and the photo.

I am at another fork in the road. It is here I make another choice.

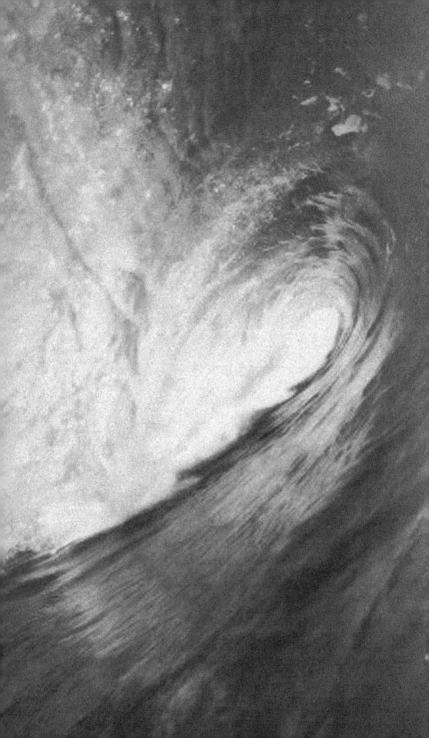

AUSTRALIA

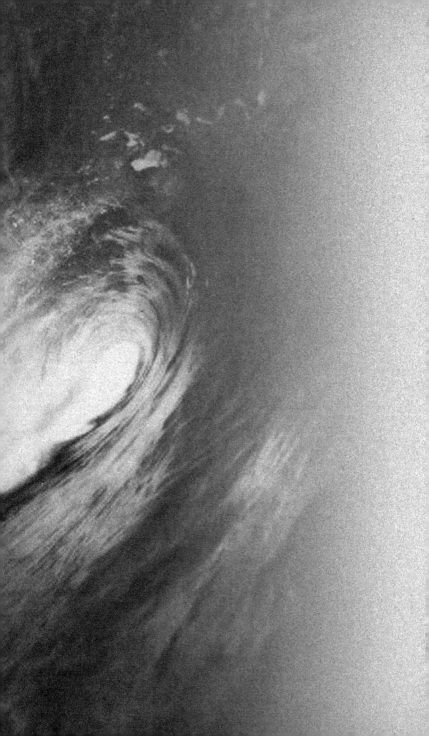

14 The final dream

The place hasn't changed much in a year and a half. The lavender hedge is gone and there are heavy tyre ruts, like canals, in the dirt driveway. Mum's old Corolla is still there, its sills nearly rusted through and the wheels in need of retreads.

She is at the kitchen table when I knock on the front door. I can see her through the pebble glass, her watery silhouette sipping at a cup. Drifting down the corridor takes her a year; she reaches out and brushes the wallpaper with her fingertips as she comes. When she opens the door, she is wearing a summer dress even though it's ten degrees outside. She is wearing pink lipstick and I can see her gulping down her want-to tears.

'I'm home, Mum,' I say, pointing at myself. Like she wouldn't have guessed by now.

'Oh, Googsy,' she says and pulls me into her arms. I smell

her perfume and the familiarity of it makes my eyes sting. She grabs my shoulders and holds me at arms length.

'Mum.'

'Yes.'

'You're kinda hurting my arm.'

She lets go. 'What's wrong with it?' she asks.

'Nothing much.'

She looks at me sideways. 'Goog.' I hate that voice. She rolls up my sleeve. 'Goog!'

'I can keep it covered. And it doesn't really hurt. Much.' I feel like I am six years old.

'But a tattoo, Goog. Remember when you and Castro . . .' She stops, but his name hangs in the air like fog. 'I guess it's okay. I mean it's not that big. And it's not a naked woman or anything.'

'That was my second choice.'

'What is it exactly?'

I look at the tatt. It's kind of scabby still, red and lumpy round the edges. 'It's a shadow puppet. *Wayang kulit.*'

Mum smiles. 'I don't mind it that much,' she says.

We go into the kitchen and I make tea and toast and we sit staring at each other across the table. I don't know what to say. Where to start.

'So?' says Mum.

'It was good,' I say. 'Yeah, the trip was real good.'

'That's nice.' She takes a sip of tea and reaches for her smokes.

'I saw Dad,' I say, as if it was the most normal thing that happened, ever.

She flinches, studies her smoke packet. 'That would've been nice.' I don't think she really heard what I said. Or she didn't take it in.

'It was shit, actually,' I say.

'Goog,' she says. 'Language.'

'Well it was, Mum. It was shit. He's some kind of rebel leader and he's living on this island shaped like a rhino and he abandoned me. Again!'

Mum smiles at me like I am on drugs and not to be trusted. 'Your dad, Goog? Really?' She purses her lips and puts her cool hand on mine. 'You've had a hard time, what with Castro disappearing and all. You should just take it easy.'

We sit staring into our cups for a while. I read my leaves – see a shark and a bunch of clouds that could be hiding Beck.

'I saw Marcella the other day,' says Mum.

'Yeah.'

'She was down from uni. Term break or something. Got herself engaged. To a lawyer.' Mum raises her eyebrows as if to say, *see if you'd stayed with her, you could have been a lawyer by now*.

'I met a girl,' I say.

'That's great, Goog. Where is she?'

'I dunno. Lost her in Sumbawa.'

'That was a bit careless,' she says and smiles.

I smile back. 'Her name was Beck. Is Beck.'

'What kind of a name is that?'

What kind of a name is Goog? 'She's from South Africa.'

'You're not thinking of taking off again are you?'

'No, Mum. Not right now.'

'Goog?'

'Yeah?'

She swallows. 'You know Castro's dad.'

'Yeah. Big bloke, drives a truck.'

'Funny, Goog. Well . . .' Mum takes out a cigarette and looks at it. 'Trying to give these up, Tony hates them,' she says and twists it under her nose like a cigar.

'Why would Castro's dad care if you smoke or not?'

'Well . . . we're sort of seeing each other.'

'Mum, you can't!'

'Why not?'

'You just can't. It's like incest, you and Mr Fidle.'

'Don't be ridiculous, Goog.'

'Don't you think you need more time? You're hardly over Dad.'

Mum sits up very straight in her chair. 'Nine years – it's enough. Time to move on.'

'But Castro's dad, Mum!'

'Tony is a good man.'

'Shit, Mum, *good man*! He's not a used car. What are you thinking?'

'Goog, that's the end of it. Don't I deserve a little happiness?'

I suppose she does deserve a little happiness. Dad is never coming home.

'Aldo turned up you know,' says Mum, changing the subject by dropping another bomb.

'Where?'

'Here. Torquay. Rolled in one day. All strange. I mean stranger than normal. Wearing a double-breasted suit. He'd lost everything else. No car, no board, nothing. He's living up in Melbourne with his Uncle Dougie if you want to catch up.'

'Yeah, maybe.' Fat chance. One year apart won't have changed him, he'll still be an arsehole. But at least he made it home from wherever Jasper dumped him, even if he did float straight back to his Nazi uncle.

'Where's Priya?' I ask.

'School.'

'How's she doing?'

'Good.'

I want to tell Mum all about my trip. How it has changed me. But I can't sit here under our Mickey Mouse clock and tell her how I hunted whales and climbed a volcano and swam in its lake and was robbed and shipwrecked and shot at, and especially how I drank the water and survived. It is all there, but I don't think she will believe any of it because it is so unlike Torquay that it may as well have happened on another planet. We have stopped understanding each other's language.

On a bench outside the surf club, I read the postcard. There is a *wayang* puppet on the front. And in gold letters: *Greetings From Jakarta.*

> *hey goog*
> *what a trip, eh? i am flying home tomorrow.*
> *max caught up with me. who would believe you*
> *and me were on the same road after all. sorry*
> *you didn't find castro. i am sure he will turn up.*
> *remember what granny said in bajawa! mind*
> *you she was a crazy old coot. guess who i saw*
> *yesterday? beck!! write back to me, man. i miss*
> *the times we had.*
> *niagara ulverstone falls.*
> *ps belacan says woof!*

I pull my own card from my pocket and force my cold-stung fingers around a pen. I keep the writing small. I have a lot to fit on the back of this small picture of Torquay.

> *Hi Niags,*
> *We did have some great times didn't we! I surfed*
> *Castro's waves and learned to open up and trust*
> *people. If I'd done that with you at the start we*
> *might have figured out our dads knew each other*
> *in Vietnam – that we were travelling the same*
> *road. We had more in common than I ever would*

have thought. I guess even though I was looking
for Castro in Indonesia I have been searching for
my father since the day he left. You were a good
friend. I know that now. Beck told me I should live
in the moment, stop wishing for what I don't have.
That is what I am going to do from today. I miss
her. I am glad you found your dad. He really cares
about you. Torquay seems small and empty.
Sometimes I think I can smell clove smoke.
Write back, man
Goog

Mad Alice is at the plaza. She is battling gulls for the grizzled remains of cold, fatty chips and stale burger buns. It is midweek, winter, getting dark. Everything is shut tight. Her plastic bag collection has grown in a year. I post my card to Niags then drift over and slip a present into her trolley. It's a shadow puppet. To someone who creates clothing from shopping bags and talks to clouds, a being that is half shadow, half light should come as no surprise.

'How are you, Alice?' I ask her.

She looks at me like she knows who I am. There is no way she remembers. 'goodgoodyupyupgood gotsomegoodstuff yup.' She hands me a flower that was once a paper napkin. 'issapresentforyou.'

I cup the flower in my hand. 'Been gone for over a year, Alice.'

She tilts her head to one side as if she is picking up another frequency.

'Went west, then up to Indo. Met a guy called Niagara Falls in Timor. We caught a bloody shark from a whaleboat. A shark, Alice! Niags had this dog called Belacan – that's Indonesian for prawn paste. He was a smelly little bugger at first but he turned out a great little four-foot.'

Alice whispers through her fingers, a little wind-song. I know she is listening.

'I surfed *Lakey*'s and nearly died. It was Niagara's fault but, hey, shit happens. Nearly died of some water thing too. That was way bad. Met a girl in Komodo. Lost her in Sumbawa. That hurt. Climbed a volcano in Lombok. Swam in its crater-lake and nearly copped parasites in my liver. Got robbed by two hooded guys. They got everything, my pack, my passport. I only had my board and my rashie, plus the clothes I stood up in.'

A dog waddles up, wagging its thick winter tail. Alice threads a drinking straw through its collar and kisses it gently on the nose. It wanders off.

I keep going. 'Did Bali. Kuta's not much, I can tell you. Saw a weird shadow puppet play in Java. Danced with a sea goddess off the coast. Could have drowned but got washed up instead.'

Alice whistles after the dog but it is nosing in the rubbish bin.

'Caught a rebel boat to a rhinoceros island but the boat

burned and sank and I had to swim for it. Surfed a gnarly reef at night. Crazy shit. But the maddest thing of all was my dad was there. On the island! Turns out, he was behind it all along – him and this guy called Jasper – plotting to get me to come up to Indo to see him.' Across from the plaza, cars are trawling up and down the main street. 'I always wished he was more of a dad but I'm never going to change him, might as well face up to it.'

I shrug and Alice sighs softly.

'At the end of it all,' I continue, 'the island got blown to shit and my worst enemy got me home. Jasper had been pulling the strings since Australia. Lured me to Indonesia with the promise of Castro. Had me and Niagara chasing separate ghosts through the islands.'

Alice doesn't look like she'll make the winter. *All bone, no meat*, Mum would say. It's cold here when the sun forgets to do its thing.

'Didn't manage to catch up with my dead friend, though,' I say. 'I didn't find Castro.'

I look at Alice. She is nodding, but she is looking at the sky.

'Missed the old place. Who would've thought it, eh? Sometimes you really don't know what you got until it's gone. You know that old song – the Joni Mitchell one.' I hum the tune as Alice kisses the wind.

'It's good to be back. But to what? I feel empty coming home like this, no photos, no souvenirs. I even lost my board.

Dad is probably cutting sick on some coral reef with it right now. I kind of miss that board.'

I rub my face hard with my travel-rough hands. 'You know what you got when you finish a circle, Alice? When you come right round in a big arc and end up at the beginning?' I hold up my hand, my thumb and forefinger pinched together to form that circle. 'You got zero, Alice. Bugger all.'

Alice smiles. She has crooked stump teeth and fish bait breath but it is the sweetest smile I have ever seen. She moves her body in a secret rhythm, a water rhythm like waves over sand.

'surfing,' she says and nods.

And with that simple word I remember what I will always have. Even when everything goes wrong and the whole land-based shitfight is against me I can escape to sea and forget about everything. I can't buy it, or trade it, or lose it. No one can steal it. It is mine forever.

I go surfing up in the corner like we used to. On my ancient six-three pintail. I found it in the shed under a stack of silverfished *Woman's Days*. I always knew this shitheap was there but before today I would've gone without a wave rather than suffer the embarrassment of paddling it into the line-up.

It's not a big day but there is a bit of swell wrapping in. *Bird Rock* is happening in a cross-shore, three-foot sort of way but it's jammed with grommies on esky lids. They are wagging period seven maths and geography, just like we used to. Me and Castro.

I am alone here because this is not a spot for surfing but for remembering.

There is an orange container ship crunching over the horizon. The sky is soapy grey and the ocean is like a scrubbed pot. The water is completely icebox. I had forgotten how ball-achingly freezing it could be. I have been spoilt with warm water for two months.

We used to surf here all year round. We put up with the city kids during the summer and the cold in midwinter. We rarely got it good. But it was ours. This square of ocean, we owned it. Or maybe it owned us.

Castro said when he got rich he'd buy the cliff and put up a big house so we could eat Coco Pops and watch the surf.

But his dreams got too big and he dreamed himself away. He ended up going too far for me to follow.

Me, I was always happy with the clifftop dream. I loved this corner. And I still do.

A small one trickles in and I paddle for it. I am slow and clumsy on this old clunker. I used to think it was the best. When we first got it home, Dad and I scraped off the deck with hot water, waxed it with a brand new block of Dr Zogg's.

I run my hands over the rails. There is an old scar near the nose where I touched the reef on my first wave at *Winki*. We were too young, but Castro was keen as. He laughed himself sick when I copped that eat. Dad cut a block of foam and glassed in the ding for me. Priya jabbed her finger in it when it was still wet; I can still see the mark.

I jump off the board and sit neck deep in the cold water so I can read the bottom. Here is my history. 'AC/DC ROCKZ' in black texta along the stringer. 'Bird Rock Boyz' near the fin. And the days we got it good: '★★★★ Steps 26/1/93, ★★★ The Bowl 14/03/94, ★★★★ Pyramid Rock 29/6/94'.

In the sharp curve of the tail: 'Goog 'n' Castro rule!'

All my memories are here and everyone knows me. It's comforting to belong. That is what this small town has to offer that nowhere else can. That is why I will stay and make something of what I have. Travelling has made me stronger; allowed me to sort out some shit. Now I can get on with things. Maybe even get back to the camera. Do that course I always said I was going to do.

I flip my board over again and sit on it. I am shivering. A breeze has sprung up and the bodyboarders are paddling in. I lie flat on the deck to escape the wind.

Seventeen days ago, I was stranded on Pulau Badak. Sixteen days ago I was with Jasper in the jungle of Sumatra. Two weeks ago I came home.

I reach into the sleeve of my wetsuit and pull it out – the card that Castro left for me on the summit of Gunung Rinjani. I remember how I felt on top of the world, looking down on the islands mapped out below. Behind to Sumbawa where I had been and ahead to Bali where I was going. It would be so simple if you could just rise up above your life like that and see the whole plan of it spread out below. To have that certainty of where you were going. Just once.

But, maybe that would take away what is best about life – not knowing what is waiting for you round the corner, over the next hill, across a wild ocean.

Pushing the card under the water, I wait until the paper is soaked through and then let it drift down. It turns over and I catch a flash of Castro's long looping handwriting. As it drifts out of sight I have a sudden urge to dive after it; to rescue the final solid bit of Castro. But I let it go. I stop looking.

I suddenly feel very tired, as if the weight of the past two and a half months, the past year and a half, has fallen onto me. I press my cheek to my board and listen to the familiar knock of the waves. It is slow and rhythmic like the music at a *wayang kulit* performance.

He paddles over like it is yesterday. Like nothing has happened and we are ten again.

'Race you to the horizon,' he says and smiles his too-big-for-the-world smile.

Acknowledgements

This book is possible because of the following people: my family – who give me dreams and space to write; Jenny Pausacker, my Tin Pot Cafe oracle; Helen Pausacker and her book *Behind the Shadows: Understanding a Wayang Performance*; Steve Beck – patron of the arts and good friend; Simon Ashford, my surf guru; Erica Wagner, Jodie Webster and Penni Russon – who love words and believed in this book; Herbert Hamilton – Swedish translator.

And the people of Lembata, Flores, Sumbawa, Lombok, Bali and Java who are more wonderfully eccentric in real life than they will ever be in fiction.